ANGELA M. SANDERS

The Halston Hit

WIDOW'S KISS

Printed in the United States of America.

First Printing, 2016

ISBN 978-0-9904133-7-0

Widow's Kiss
P.O. Box 82488
Portland, OR 97282

www.WidowsKiss.com

Book design: Eric Lancaster

*This book is dedicated to those of you
with the courage to live the real you.
Don't ever change.*

The Halston Hit

Chapter 1

Joanna held up two halves of a child's foam basketball, each covered in pantyhose. "Is this what you're looking for?"

"Hand them here." Vintage Chablis tucked each half into the top of her strapless gown and adjusted them. "There. A perfect C cup. What do you think?" The drag queen raised her chin and regarded herself in the mirror. Gold silk jersey gathered across her chest, then flowed, Grecian-style, to her signature leopard print heels. "I look killer."

"In that Halston, you should." Finding a suitable dress—Vintage Chablis wore only vintage—that fit a tall girl had been a challenge. Finding a Halston was a real coup, even for an experienced vintage clothing boutique owner like Joanna.

"Maybe you should keep this one. Could be your wedding dress," VC said, still preening.

"For a day wedding? I don't think so. Besides, I have to get it to Penny tomorrow." A gentle hand wash and overnight air dry should do the trick. "Careful with that foundation."

VC paused, a stick of foundation slightly darker than her cocoa-hued skin in hand. "Hush, child. I've made up a few thousand faces in my time, remember."

Joanna laughed. Those faces had been customers of VC's family's funeral home. "At least you're not dealing with the victim of a coronary this time."

"Narrowly. Hand Vintage Chablis her wig, honey."

Joanna lifted a platinum wig in a sleek bob from the stand behind her. A palm-sized pink silk hibiscus was already clipped to its crown. "This one?"

"Perfect." She pulled the wig over her shaved head, then swore, yanking it off. She pressed a finger to her scalp and showed it to Joanna. Blood.

Joanna handed her a tissue. "What happened?"

"Something sharp." VC slid a long, pearl-tipped pin from the wig. "Look at that." Her eyes narrowed. "Caramella. That witch. She'll pay for this." VC placed the wig on her head again, then turned toward the other performers. "Girl," she shouted at another drag queen halfway down the long dressing table. "I know what you did."

"What are you talking about?" Caramella set down her russet lip liner and swiveled to meet VC's challenging gaze.

The drag queens, one seated, a smirk on her face, and one tall in leopard stilettos, squared off. The other queens, in varying states of dress, paused to watch.

"You put this pin in my wig." VC's voice had deepened to a growl. She held the pin aloft, then stabbed it into the poison green velvet dress hanging behind her. "You're sabotaging me."

"Persecution complex." Caramella returned to her task. Lips now lined, she turned a cheek to clip dangling rhinestones to one ear as part of a costume that appeared to be part Annie Oakley and part bordello madam.

VC snatched the cowboy hat from Caramella's head, taking her wig of pale pink curls with it.

"Give that back!" Caramella shot from her stool and grabbed at

VC's wig, knocking the attached silk flower to the floor. Joanna picked it up before one of them stepped on it.

"VC in two," the intercom crackled. The music switched to a rolling disco beat. It vibrated from the stage above, buzzing in the light fixtures.

"Shoot. I'm up." The queens backed slowly away from each other.

"Your flower," Joanna said. She might as well not have spoken. All attention was focused on the combatants. She tucked the hibiscus in her bag.

VC pointed a shellacked finger at Caramella. "Later," she threatened, finally breaking eye contact and strutting past the other girls.

Joanna followed VC through the greasy kitchen, where the cook, a mole-like man, lifted a basket of onion rings from the fryer. They mounted the narrow staircase to the theater's main level. When VC emerged from the stairwell, she lit up, as if the melee downstairs had never happened.

"Wish me luck." VC sashayed to the stage, waving at the audience. Her charisma washed to the room's corners.

Impressed by VC's ability to shift to entertainer mode, Joanna blew her a kiss.

Joanna stayed at the back of the room and leaned against the wall. Marquise's Showplace was a small theater with a sound system given to static and a vaguely Victorian decorating scheme heavy on velvet swags. Rows of chairs lined the center, and waiters delivered vodka sodas and baskets of chicken fingers to patrons. Red vinyl banquettes anchored the rear. At one, judges for La Fille Fantastique scribbled notes.

This was Portland's most important drag queen pageant. Tonight's winner would advance to La Fille Fantastique International. The theater's owner, a long-time Portland celebrity, Marquise, was in his mid-eighties and insisted on early showtimes, but even so, pageants could go on for hours. This one had kicked off at five, and it might last until midnight. Joanna hadn't known this when she'd suggested she wait out VC's turn in the Halston during the talent segment so she could take the dress home right away. They'd already weathered the black-and-white outfit presentation and formal wear. After talent came the elaborate showgirl segment.

"She could win, you know." Alexis Campbell Starr, a previous winner of La Fille Fantastique Plus, the division for curvier queens, slipped next to Joanna. "Here, I got you this." She handed Joanna a highball glass.

A gin and tonic. Perfect. "Thanks." Joanna loved to stand next to drag queens. She felt so petite. "What's the deal with VC and Caramella? I thought VC was going to bean her with a curling iron down there."

Alexis, known as Austin in street clothes, raised inch-long eyelashes tipped with rhinestones. "Lord knows. It's really gotten bad over the past year. Marquise had a talk with them over Christmas, but things only got worse."

On stage, VC lip synced about boogie woogie dancing shoes making her queen for the night. The audience — even the bachelorette party with umbrella-studded drinks — sat rapt. It was as if VC had a built-in switch. When she flipped it, she illuminated the room with palpable light. You were powerless but to watch.

"Could you please find me a Halston, too?" Alexis whispered. "Pretty please?"

"Not likely. To get this one, I had to trade an Ossie Clark with a dealer in Las Vegas."

VC bowed to thunderous applause. She strode off the stage, hips swaying, and Joanna moved to join her.

Alexis hooked Joanna's arm. "Stay here. Why not enjoy the show a moment?"

"Won't VC need help with the showgirl costume? The headdress is gigantic."

"She's been dressing herself for years."

Joanna leaned against the wall again. She did have most of her drink left, after all. "All right. I guess a few minutes won't make a difference."

"What do you think of all this?" Alexis asked. "I mean, the vibe has to be different than you're used to."

"True." At Tallulah's Closet, her vintage clothing store, clients tended to be serious "I wear nothing but vintage" types, or romantics with a love of old movies. Here, the look was straight-up, hyperbolized glamour. Intentional and calculated. Each performer chose a persona and a style, and that style usually bucked *Vogue* magazine's dictates of what women should be wearing. "But it's authentic. In some ways, it feels more real than what happens in the West Hills," she said, referring to one of Portland's old money neighborhoods. "Everyone has her own personality."

Alexis nodded toward the stage. "Caramella's up. This should be good. I think she wants to beat VC more than she wants the crown."

The sound system switched to a sultry blues number. Not what drag queens usually chose. Caramella sauntered to the stage, moving to the music's rolling two-four rhythm. Now Joanna remembered the song: "Frankie and Johnny." That explained the cowboy get-up. Caramella had added a marabou-trimmed vest to her outfit and tidied her wig and hat. Why did Caramella and VC detest each other so much? Tallulah's Closet served a number of drag queens, and despite clichés about catfights, Joanna had always admired their camaraderie.

The song's hypnotic roll lulled Joanna into the first calm she'd felt all night. But when it came to "he did her wrong," the drag queen yanked a toy pistol from her holster and pulled the trigger. The shot exploded through the theater, the sound system screaming in protest. The bachelorette party shrieked. A waiter nearly lost a tray of drinks.

Alexis patted Joanna's arm. "No worries. It's part of the tape. She warned us. Clever, actually, although maybe a bit loud."

Joanna sucked in her breath to ease the pulse that jackhammered in her ears. "No kidding. You should have paramedics standing by." She handed Alexis her glass. "I'm going to check on VC, see if she needs my help."

Joanna returned down the stairway and through the kitchen, where the cook sipped ice water from a pint glass. He didn't move, but his gaze followed her as she passed. The kitchen led into the dressing room. On the left ran the dressing table, a long counter with light-studded mirrors and eight stools tucked beneath it.

VC wasn't at the dressing table—no one was, in fact—but she wasn't surprised. The costume's feathered wings were so large that she likely went around the corner where there was more room.

"VC, are you ready? You're up next," Joanna said. "I'll pack the Halston."

No reply. Joanna wrinkled her brow. VC's showgirl outfit, a white pants suit sparkling with Swarovski crystals, still hung against the wall. This wasn't like her. She was a professional. She'd talked about gluing heart-shaped rhinestones to her cheeks. Maybe it was taking longer than she'd expected.

"You're going to have to hurry. I'll help." Joanna passed by the dressing table, the gowns hanging opposite brushing her shoulders. She rounded the corner and opened her mouth to urge VC to get a move on. Her jaw clamped shut again. VC was lying face down. Blood made a scarlet halo on the cement floor.

"VC." Joanna's voice cracked. *No no no.* She turned toward the door, frantic for help, before forcing herself to face the drag queen again. *Calm down.* Maybe she passed out and bloodied her nose, that's all. Joanna sucked in a deep breath and rolled the body over. She staggered back, grabbing the edge of a table.

There was nothing left of the drag queen's face.

Chapter 2

Cold shivers prickled Joanna's arms and back. An almost animal response to flee overtook her, and she turned away from the body. And then, something strange: calm. Shock squelched all emotion. It might not last long. She stood straight. She had to find a phone.

A group of clumsy uniformed policemen weren't going to get anything useful from the performers, and she knew it. She'd call homicide detective Foster Crisp. Crisp might not glean much, either, but with his almost freakishly unflappable manner, he stood a better chance.

"Vintage Chablis," Strawberry Crush's runner, a skinny African-American boy, yelled from the front dressing area. "Show girl number!"

Joanna's hand trembled only a little as she pulled a rolling rack of costumes between the dressing rooms and where VC lay to hide the body. "She can't make it. She's—she's not well."

The runner stared at Joanna. "It's the showgirl number. She has to."

"She can't make it."

"She'd have to be in her grave before—" The runner's eyes widened. "That's her feet."

She could not let them trample evidence. There was no way she could keep people out of the main dressing room. In fact, she heard another of the performers entering to change costumes as they spoke.

But she could shield where VC lay. "Listen," Joanna whispered. "This is important. Tell Marquise that VC twisted her ankle or something. And no one is to come down here except the police. Stand at the top of the stairs, if you have to. Can you do that?"

Attention rapt, he nodded.

She swallowed. "Do you know where I can find a phone?"

The boy pulled an immaculate smartphone from his dingy pocket. One benefit of Luddite ways was that she didn't rely on devices to remember phone numbers. She punched in Detective Crisp's personal cell phone number.

The runner paused a second before darting through the narrow dressing room toward the kitchen, the basement's only outlet to upstairs. Despite the strange phone number that must have appeared on his caller ID — or maybe because of it — Crisp answered.

"It's Joanna Hayworth. I found a body. You've got to get down here."

"Slow down. Where are you?"

"At Marquise's Showplace in Old Town. It's awful." The shock was fading. "They blew off her face."

"Are you safe?"

She couldn't talk. VC's tropicana-style music faded, and a rumba beat tattooed through the floorboards. The metallic scent of blood mingled with the smells of fried food and makeup.

"Joanna? Listen. Stay put. I'll be right there."

She hung up and set the phone aside. She squeezed her eyes shut, then opened them and forced herself to take in the scene. VC lay face down on the floor. On one side of her body, her showgirl headdress with unmarred white feathers rested on a table. At her feet was a closed wardrobe with a mirrored front. On the other side, completing a U-shape, was a shelf of wigs on styrofoam heads staring at the macabre scene. Judging from her face's devastation, VC had to have been shot point-blank.

Who did it? Caramella's trick during the Western number upstairs would have covered the gunfire that killed VC. But Caramella had been upstairs and couldn't have shot VC through the floor.

No, it had to have happened right here. Joanna scanned the basement. The long, narrow dressing area ran along the wall, filling a quarter of the room. Shelves, many with dresses hooked to their sides, screened the dressing room from the rest of the basement, which was full of racks of dresses—Marquise's archive of show gowns.

VC lay near the basement's east wall, past the long dressing table and just beyond where the shelves ended. It wasn't lit well, but there was more room here to put on the headdress and wings her showgirl costume required.

The cook would have had to have seen the murderer on the way in—and out. Unless—all at once the sounds of the show upstairs receded and Joanna's own heartbeat throbbed in her ears—unless the killer was still down here. He could have waited for hours among Marquise's gowns. No one would have known.

Her senses focused. Aside from muffled music above, the HVAC system's humming was the only noise. Faintly, she heard the fryer basket plunged into fat in the kitchen. She was alone. *Maybe.* She gripped the dressing table's edge with clammy palms and flattened her body against a support pillar. She pulled a gold sequined stiletto off the shelf as a weapon. A minute passed, then two. She strained to hear any sound betraying another presence in the basement's darkened area, but it was silent.

At last the sound of quick, sure steps through the dressing room told her Crisp had arrived. "Joanna," he said. "Where?"

Tension drained out of her, leaving her limp as a stocking. She pushed back the rack of gowns to reveal VC's body but kept her head turned away. "I rolled her face up to make sure she was—"

Before she finished her sentence, Crisp was on the phone demanding backup. He hung up. "Next time call 911. I'll find my way here if I'm needed."

"It's kind of a delicate situation." The performers wouldn't talk to just anyone. They'd already made a few pointed remarks about the police. VC had told her officers had even stopped some of the queens after the show a few weeks ago and questioned them for no apparent reason.

"That's the only entrance?" He gestured toward the kitchen.

"As far as I know. I haven't said anything to the cook." She dropped her voice. "There's still the chance he's here."

She didn't need to tell Crisp who "he" was. The detective drew a handgun from under his western-cut jacket. Joanna had the ridiculous thought that Caramella could have used him—cowboy boots, bolo tie, and all—in her talent number.

"What's going on here?" Marquise, her cotton candy-styled wig towering, appeared from the dressing area, the runner at her back.

"Sit down," Crisp commanded. "You," he said to the runner. "Guard the entrance."

Joanna shook her head. Crisp would get nowhere with that attitude.

The runner glanced at Marquise, and on receiving a nod, turned to Joanna. "Can I have my phone?" Joanna, eyes still on Crisp, handed it to him.

The detective edged toward the other side of the basement's dividing wall. He flipped three light switches at once. Fluorescent tubes flickered to life, flooding the area in blue light. Nothing moved.

"VC," Marquise said. She'd ignored Crisp's warning and stood over the body. "Darling girl." Her hem dragged through the blood, and even through thick face powder her face blanched, then reddened. She raised her head, and with the full force of decades on stage, shouted, "Who did this?"

"Shut up," Crisp commanded.

Marquise responded with a stare that lowered the room's temperature ten degrees. Joanna winced. Marquise deserved more respect than that.

Crisp crept around the corner. Clothing racks on wheels crammed with ruffles, chiffon, and sequins filled most of the room. Marquise was not petite, and neither were her dresses. An army of murderers could hide there.

Holding his gun steady, Crisp pushed one rack with his whole body, sending it careening into the other racks like lace-pouffed dominoes. The racks rolled and scattered, some hitting the walls. No one was there. The cement floor was surprisingly clean. A few rat traps, empty, rested at regular intervals along the dividing row of shelves.

Marquise sat at her dressing table stool, lips clamped shut. It was clear that only pure will kept her from returning to her feet.

"We're good," Crisp said.

"Here's Marquise," Joanna said. "She'll be able to help." Joanna begged the detective with her eyes to apologize. Calling Crisp had been a mistake. Any random homicide detective would have had enough sense not to antagonize potential witnesses.

Crisp ignored her as four uniformed cops filed into the dressing room. "Clear the audience," Crisp told them. "Get everyone's contact information, then let them go. The performers and staff stay. And the cook. I'll talk to him first."

"Perhaps I can help," Marquise said, her voice even. The elderly queen was a gentleman, but her nostrils flared slightly, and her gaze hardened. No one gives orders in my theater, it seemed to say.

"I'll tell you when I need you." Crisp didn't even make eye contact.

Joanna edged toward Marquise. "It'll be all right. Not easy for any of us, but VC...." She nodded toward the floor behind the dressing table. "We don't have a choice."

Marquise leaned her neck forward, then closed her eyes and looked away. She crossed herself.

*
**

An hour later, the theater was empty but for two waiters, the cook, and nine sullen men in demi-drag occupying a row in the audience. Three of them passed a vodka bottle, and two held wigs in their laps. Crisp left the two officers taking statements and led Joanna back downstairs for questioning.

Crisp steered her to Marquise's office, away from the crime scene specialists tending to VC's body, and pointed to an oak office chair with wheels. She sat and took in the room. A wooden desk was pushed against one wall, and an armless oak office chair, the one Crisp occupied, sat nearby. A rain jacket hung from a coat rack. The jacket looked like something an older man would wear — conservative cut, probably ten or fifteen years old — a reminder that Marquise was also a grandfather. A movie poster advertising *Mommie Dearest* was taped to the drywall behind the coat rack.

"Start from the beginning," was all Crisp said.

Joanna and Crisp had met because of a body Joanna had found at her boutique a year and a half before. Back then, Crisp didn't trust her.

They'd come to a mutual understanding—and respect—since then.

"You're messing this up," Joanna said. "With your attitude, they won't tell you anything. You can't bully drag queens."

"Never mind that. Tell me what you saw. What brought you to Marquise's, anyway?"

She told him how she'd met Bo Milton, also known as Vintage Chablis, through Summer Seasons, one of the drag queens who regularly patrolled her shop for pieces to complement their costumes. Lately, VC had stopped by with crazy ideas for Joanna's wedding: a pasha on a camel for the reception; a bouquet of feathers instead of flowers; a soundtrack of disco favorites.

For tonight's pageant, she'd lent VC a valuable Halston evening gown, something she never would have done for a customer she didn't know and trust—or care about, frankly. She'd stayed around to take it back to the shop later, to hand wash it so it would be ready to hand off the next day.

"Tonight. What time did you arrive?" Crisp said.

Joanna filled Crisp in on what she'd seen of the show, and how she came downstairs to help VC with her headdress for the showgirl number. As she talked, she walked through the scenario in her mind, her steps through the dressing room, what she saw, what she heard.

"Anything else?" Crisp asked.

"The only entrance to the basement is through the kitchen. The cook would have seen everyone who came through."

"If he was paying attention. The house was full, and he had orders to fill," Crisp said.

"Plus, the girls and their runners would have been going up and down all evening."

"That's what he said. Told me he doesn't even notice anymore, his kitchen is overrun with strangers. He seemed a little resentful."

"But VC? He wasn't upset about her death?"

"He was upset, all right." Crisp leaned to brush something from his lizard-tipped cowboy boots. "He seemed more upset by the attention it would bring to Marquise's than anything else."

"He's an odd one," she said absently.

Crisp leaned back in his chair. "I'm surprised there isn't another entrance straight to backstage."

"I know," Joanna said. "It would make sense. It's an old building. I guess 'code' meant something different then."

"Maybe there's an entrance through the shanghai tunnels," Crisp said.

"You aren't serious?" Rumor had it that a network of tunnels running underneath Old Town had been used to kidnap drunk tavern patrons to sell to crew-hungry ship captains, but that myth had been debunked years ago. Regardless, tourists lined up to visit unfinished basements where liquor had been stored during Prohibition and the Chinese had maintained gambling operations a century earlier.

"No entrances down here. Nothing obvious, at least. That's it, then?" Crisp said.

"Well, there's one more thing. VC had some sort of running feud with Caramella, another of the performers. She was onstage when VC was killed. She did a routine to the old song "Frankie and Johnny." Joanna looked up to see if Crisp knew that one. He nodded. "At one point during the song, she shot into the air, and she'd edited the sound of a gunshot into the tape. A loud one."

"You think it could have been coordinated to cover the sound of the shot?"

"Maybe. She would have known VC was downstairs changing

costumes. Alexis—one of Marquise's performers—said they were all warned about the sound effects."

Crisp appeared to think it over. "It's possible. The ceiling isn't soundproof. But it could be a coincidence, too. With the audience and the music, no one would have heard a firearm with a silencer. Do you know what the conflict was about?"

Joanna shook her head. "VC wouldn't talk about it. Said it was beneath her notice."

Crisp stood. "We'll see about that. That's all?"

"Not quite." Crisp was used to barking commands and getting his way. That wasn't going to work here.

He waited. Last year, he would have been annoyed. "Go on."

"Your attitude tonight is alienating Marquise and the girls. I can see it in how they won't make eye contact with you. You're on their turf."

"They're getting the same respect we give everyone. Why should they be different?"

"I've heard a few of the girls say that the police haven't been treating them fairly, that they're getting harassed. What's going on?"

"What do you mean?"

"Officers have been parked outside, and a few of the girls have been pulled aside and questioned."

Crisp made a note. "It hasn't come up in homicide. I'll look into it."

She pulled his arm as he made to leave. "Promise me you'll be more respectful."

"Come on." This time he pulled away.

Upstairs, nothing had changed but the level of the vodka bottle's contents.

"They won't say anything," a policeman told Crisp. "Nothing."

"There's nothing to tell," said one of the queens—Sunset Blush,

Joanna thought her name was. "We did our show. The pageant was going along fine, then this."

"Which one of you is Caramella?" Crisp asked. He stood with his feet shoulder-width, looking strangely at home in the theater. Both he and the theater could have been transported from a Mae West movie.

"That's me, officer." Caramella handed the vodka bottle to the girl next to her. She had been dressed for the showgirl segment. Her massive head dress and shoulder piece leaned against the wall shedding orange feathers. Orange fluff stuck to her sequined leotard.

"I understand you and the deceased didn't get along."

"The deceased," Caramella said. "Listen to the sheriff."

"Bo Milton," Crisp said. "Vintage Chablis."

"I don't know what you're talking about. We've worked together for simply ages." The drag queen mopped her crocodile tears with a paper napkin. "I'm all torn up about her death."

Caramella's emotional outburst was clearly an act, but Joanna swore she saw something deeper in her trembling hand. Did she care about VC more than she let on? Or maybe it was fear. Or guilt.

Joanna's own emotional exhaustion must have shown in her face, because Marquise, now a man dressed in a terrycloth robe, his wig removed, set a hand on her shoulder. "Honey," he said, "you've had a tough evening. I'm sorry."

"We've all had a tough evening," she said. Marquise was a kind, kind man. She understood why his performers were so loyal to him. "Can I go home now?" she whispered to Crisp.

The vodka bottle traveled once more down the row of drag queens.

"Fine," Crisp said. "I'll catch up with you later. It's going to be a long night."

Chapter

Tallulah's Closet wasn't due to open for another hour, but Joanna came in early. She'd had a restless night, seeing VC's lifeless foot with its leopard stiletto askew every time she closed her eyes. Paul couldn't help much. He'd tried, bringing her a tiny, frosty martini, but it tasted like ashes. She'd read from *Pride and Prejudice* before bed, but the familiar words didn't give their usual comfort. Crisp is going to mess this up, she kept thinking. Unless he could solve the case on forensic evidence alone, he was screwed.

Spending time at Tallulah's Closet would calm her. She'd spent eight-plus years making the shop into her approximation of a starlet's dressing room, complete with velvet-upholstered furniture, brocade draperies tying off the dressing rooms, and even a chandelier. A few funky touches remained: a zebra-upholstered chair awaited bored husbands, and a tiki bar was the checkout counter. If she couldn't find comfort here, at least she'd find something to do. Keeping a vintage clothing boutique going was a marathon of laundry, repairs, and finding stock.

She turned her key in the shop door, then halted. Apple, her best friend and coworker, was already there. "Good morning. What are you doing here so early?" Joanna closed the door behind her.

Apple's colorful caftan gave her the look of a gypsy. A gypsy washerwoman, that is. She was scrubbing the baseboards near the dressing rooms at the store's rear with an old washcloth. "I could ask you the same."

Joanna took a thermos from her bag. "I couldn't sleep." She told Apple about VC's death while she poured half-and-half-laced coffee into a porcelain mug painted with roses.

"Oh, no." Eyes wide, Apple tossed the rag in a bucket. "Vintage Chablis. I adored her. Oh, Joanna."

"I know. It still doesn't feel real."

"Wow." Apple shook her head. "Do they have any idea who did it?"

"None. I left Detective Crisp talking to the performers. I doubt they got very far." Joanna remembered VC complaining about the occasional unmarked—but easy to make—police sedans parked outside Marquise's. "Crisp kept ordering Marquise around, acting like he owned the place."

"Who would hurt VC, let alone kill her?" Apple said. "I mean, there must be some reason."

"I didn't hear all the questioning, but earlier VC said that another of the girls, Caramella, had it in for her. VC even found a pin in her wig and swore Caramella put it there."

"A pin is a long way from a bullet." Apple picked up a string of blue crystals and turned them in her palm, pressing the faceted beads into her flesh.

"True. There must be something behind it, though."

It had been only the week before that VC, as Bo, wandered into Tallulah's Closet for one of his biweekly perusals of her inventory. He was drawn to dresses from the 1970s, often polyester crêpe de chine and stretchy. They hung well from his broad shoulders. That day, he'd been considering the merits of a white jumpsuit that might have graced an Abba album cover when he saw the Halston hanging behind the counter.

"What's that? The gold lamé number?" he asked.

"It's for Penny to wear to some life achievement banquet for Wilson in L.A." Penny's fiancé, a musician, had died the winter before. Joanna pulled the gown from the rack and unzipped its garment bag. "A Halston."

"Magnificent." He held the gown against his body and looked in the mirror. "Absolutely killer." He hung it on a rack and examined its skirt. "It's cut on the bias, isn't it?"

"Halston's famous spiral cut. He used extra-wide lengths of fabric so he could fold it at an angle, then sew along the folds for a long spiral hem. And look"—she came around the counter and touched the simple tie across the gown's bust—"this is the dress's only fastener. No zippers or buttons."

He touched the tie reverently. "What stunning craftsmanship."

"Halston worked side by side with Charles James. You should see the layout for Halston's pinwheel gown. Amazingly complex, but it looks like nothing on the hanger."

Bo couldn't peel his gaze from the gown. "You don't think—"

"Not a chance," Joanna said. She knew where this was going. "Penny's event is a week from Tuesday."

Bo smiled shyly. Uh-oh. He was turning on the charm. He sidled to the counter. "The Fille Fantastique pageant is this weekend. Summer Seasons made me a gown, but this one would be so much nicer."

"No way. It's couture Halston. Penny already bought it. Penny's flying to L.A. Monday afternoon. There's no time."

Bo lowered his eyelashes, then gave Joanna a melting look. "Maybe I could talk to her. Wouldn't the gown be that much nicer if it helped a girl like me win the crown?"

The dress would look good on him, no doubt about it. But if anything happened to it…. "No. It's too risky, Bo."

He kept up the seductive purr in his voice. "Why don't you give her a call? All she can do is say no."

Joanna had sighed. She'd dialed Penny's number and had handed Bo the phone.

But that was last week. So much had changed since then. A gentle shudder ran over her arms and back, and she leaned against the tiki bar. Emotional exhaustion settled in, a metabolizing of the evening's shock.

"I'll have to call Penny, I guess," Joanna said.

"Are you all right?"

"Just remembering last night. I'm fine." Joanna tilted her head. "You're not getting one of your 'feelings' about the death, are you?"

"No." Apple's voice was curiously flat. She turned away.

Joanna picked up the necklace Apple had dropped on the counter and rehung it. "But you still haven't answered my question. Why are you here so early? And cleaning baseboards?"

Apple retrieved the washcloth and knelt by a baseboard. "Oh, you know."

"Know what?" Joanna could usually count on Apple to speak her mind. It was one of the reasons she so happily agreed when Apple offered to plan her and Paul's small wedding ceremony. Today she was bizarrely evasive. Not like her at all.

Apple stood suddenly. "Drat. The catering. The caterer for the wedding called last night and pulled out. She had a family emergency and has to leave town."

"Oh, no." Joanna sat down. "Does she have a backup?"

"No. She's a one-woman operation. Don't worry, though. I'll call around. It's only twenty-five people."

Joanna had chosen the caterer for her enthusiasm about using seasonal food. For lunch they'd settled on poached salmon—the Chinook run had just started—on spring greens with tiny pansies and chive tips and a huckleberry compote on the side. The caterer even had an arrangement with a Native American tribe on the Columbia for the freshest fish. Now, no lunch. She should have known. It was too good to be true.

"If worse comes to worst, MacClay's Smokehouse will make up some ribs," Joanna said.

"I do have some good news," Apple said.

"Bring it on."

"The ad I put online is getting results. Yesterday, someone brought in a wedding dress that would be perfect for you."

"This one?" Joanna lifted a garment bag from the rack behind the counter and unzipped it.

Apple took it from her hands and pulled out the dress, setting it on a rack for a better view. Alençon lace wound over an ivory chiffon skirt as thick and wide as Cinderella's ball gown. From its wide, shoulder-baring neckline and heavy boning, Joanna judged it from the late 1950s.

"Priscilla of Boston," she read the label. "I love it. An Eisenhower-era debutante's dream."

"I knew you'd appreciate it. You don't find this kind of quality every day. Look, it came with its own certificate from the dry cleaners." Apple handed her a leatherette folder with a black-and-white photo of the dress and its description, engraved. June 15, 1957.

Joanna touched the dress's bodice again, then regretfully turned away. "But it's not right for the wedding."

Apple's arms dropped. "What do you mean? You just said it's perfect."

"It *is* perfect. Perfect for a giant church wedding in the afternoon or evening. This dress is too formal for mine. It would look out of place at the B&B."

Apple shook her head. "You have six days to find a dress. Here's a lovely option. What if we save it as a backup?"

"It's not the right one. Just because it's a small wedding, there's no reason every detail can't be just right."

"Let me remind you, this is the fifth dress you've rejected."

Joanna knew she was being ridiculous. She'd made fun of picky brides who visited the store, and here she was doing the same thing. With vintage, you had to be open to serendipity and not insist on some vision of a dress you'd held since you were sixteen. The memory of VC's suggestion that she wear the Halston stabbed her momentary calm. "I just want it to be perfect. After everything I've put Paul through — " First, stand-offishness, then jealousy, not to mention a few run-ins with the Homicide Bureau.

"Yeah, you were no peach. But I hardly think that matters to him."

"He deserves it to be just right. We'll have lunch, the Mother Superior marries us, and then afternoon champagne and cocktails." She already had a case of Taittinger in the basement and a couple dozen vintage Bohemian cut crystal coupes awaiting duty. They'd rented a beautiful old bed and breakfast outside town with a wrap-around porch, shoulder-high fireplace, and a view of the mountains. Apple had made letter-pressed invitations. All that remained was the dress. Well, now the lunch, too.

"What does Paul think?"

"He says he's fine with whatever we come up with, as long as I'm there." A warm flush washed over Joanna at the thought of him.

"See? Then this dress is fine."

"Nice, but not quite perfect."

Apple tossed up her hands. "Perfect. You're using that word again. Nothing is perfect. No relationship is perfect."

Joanna shot her a glance. "Would you care to elaborate?"

"Just a figure of speech. But it's not smart to depend too much on one person." She busied herself putting the chiffon dress into its garment bag. She returned the bag to the rack behind the counter with an ostentatious clunk, and in swiveling to face Joanna, she accidentally knocked Joanna's bag to the floor.

The black alligator bag—a large Lucile of Paris, she'd taken it to Marquise's the night before—spilled open.

"I'm sorry," Apple said.

"That's fine." The women knelt to pick up its contents: a gold-toned compact, a lipstick, two crumpled handkerchiefs sprigged with flowers, an orphaned Miriam Haskell earring—

"What's this?" Apple held up a pink silk flower.

Joanna took it from her and stood. "It's VC's. It fell off her wig."

They stared at the flower. It was thickly petaled, like a fantasy take on a Hawaiian garden or something Dorothy Lamour would have worn to a disco in outer space.

"Oh, VC."

"I'm sorry, Jo. It must have been awful."

Joanna pulled a pale green chiffon scarf from a display and gently wrapped the flower. Her wedding lunch and dress faded in importance. VC's family would be drowning in grief right now.

"Her family should have this." Joanna tucked the bundle into her purse. "I'm going to take it to them."

Chapter 4

The morning was overcast but not wet, and trees were beginning to break into leaf. Joanna wanted to clear her head, so she walked the mile or so to Milton Funeral Directors, VC's family business and, from what she'd told her, home. The funeral home was in a turn-of-the-century mansion on what was now an arterial boulevard, but walking up its horseshoe driveway set in a park of old chestnut trees, Joanna imagined how quiet it must have been when downtown was a long carriage ride away.

She climbed the stairs to a broad porch and pushed open the wide oak door. For a moment, she took in the Oriental carpets, oil paintings, and antique furniture. No wonder VC had latched onto the "vintage" theme.

Despite the front door's creaking, no one greeted her. The mansion was still and smelled of old wood and furniture polish. She hesitated. Should she try to find an office?

"Sorry," said a man hurrying left from the hall, pulling on a suit jacket. "We're a bit short-handed at the moment. We, um—" He stopped. "May I help you?"

He was clearly VC's brother. Besides his tall, slender build, he had VC's full lips. He moved with less grace, though, and his handshake was firm enough to jar Joanna's arm in its socket.

"I'm Joanna Hayworth. I knew VC — I mean, Bo," she said, referring to his birth name.

"One of his drag friends?"

"I helped him with his wardrobe."

The man's face shut down. "Thank you for your condolences." He stared, as if daring her to say more.

"I'm so sorry."

A grandfather clock ticked in the hall.

VC's brother didn't move. His expression was unreadable. "If that's all, I should get back to work." He turned to leave.

"Wait. Don't go. I have something of your brother's. I thought you should have it." She'd leave the silk flower and go back to Tallulah's Closet. She didn't know what to do in the face of what seemed to be a complete lack of emotion. Maybe when you're in the funeral business, you don't grieve the same way others do.

"Honey?" a voice came from the hall.

"It's okay, Mom. I'm taking care of it."

Rounding the corner came one of the most beautiful women Joanna had ever seen. VC's mother. Had to be. She was nearly as tall as her son, and her face could have been carved into cameos for its large oval eyes, high cheekbones, and delicate nose.

Joanna shifted the chiffon-wrapped hibiscus to her left hand and repeated the handshake and introduction. She handed the bundle to VC's mother. "I was at Marquise's last night when your son passed away."

"Died. Or, more precisely, was killed." His mother's voice was matter of fact. "We know what it means."

"Yes." Again, that uncomfortable silence. "I was there last night, and…well, he left this behind."

Bo's mother untied the loose knot, and green chiffon wafted around her palm. She lifted the hibiscus as if it were a newborn kitten and touched it to her cheek. When she spoke, something had changed. Her voice was softer, warmer. "I'm Adele. Bo's mother. This is my son, Barry." She gestured toward VC's brother. "You're Joanna, you said?"

Joanna nodded.

"Come in and have a cup of coffee." It was a command, but friendly and gentle all the same.

"Mom, we're busy," Barry said.

"I'll be upstairs shortly. Delilah will be here any minute. She'll get the phone."

The brother hesitated.

"Go up," she said. "I'll be there soon enough. You need to get Mrs. Mizer ready for visitation at three." Then, to Joanna, "This way."

Joanna followed Adele past a chapel—it looked as if it had been the house's living room at one time—to a service staircase at the house's far east side. VC's mother wore a long, pewter wool tunic over matching narrow trousers. The tunic rippled as she walked, wafting a hint of vetiver. The women descended one level into an English basement kitchen with a round wooden table and gingham-sprigged curtains. It was as if they'd passed from a stuffy mansion to an entirely different world, a homey cottage.

"Have a seat." Adele pointed to a chair at the table. "Buffy, you get down from there."

A fluffy dog—a toy poodle, maybe?—leapt from the chair next to Joanna's and curled up in a dog bed in the corner.

"It's fine. I love animals," Joanna said.

"He's not supposed to be on the furniture, and he knows it." Instead of fussing at the counter for coffee, Adele sat down in the chair the dog had left. "Tell me what you know. They have Bo at the medical examiner's office. All they say is that he was murdered."

Joanna drew a deep breath. "The police haven't been to see you?"

Adele waved her hand dismissively. "They called. They're supposed to come back today. But" — she leaned forward and clenched her jaw — "he's my son."

Bo's mother's beauty was unimpeachable, but now Joanna saw the strain in her skin and eyes. She couldn't have slept much, if at all. "I have a vintage clothing store. Tallulah's Closet. As Vintage Chablis, he —" Joanna didn't know how comfortable Adele was with her son's drag queen lifestyle and wasn't sure what pronoun to use. Bo's brother evidently wasn't on board.

"She," Adele said.

"She wore vintage gowns as often as she could. Last night was La Fille Fantastique pageant. I lent her a Halston for the talent number."

Adele nodded. "Bo told me about that. Loved that dress." Her gaze wandered to the windowed back door, then to Joanna again.

"I went down after her talent performance, and I found her."

Adele seemed to force the words. "Found her how?"

"She'd been shot." She would not give Adele more detail than that. No mother deserved to picture what Joanna had seen.

Bo's mother sucked in her breath and sat up straight. "They only told me she was killed. They didn't say more."

"I'm sorry," Joanna whispered.

"Thank you, child." Adele's face was frozen into indifference, but the blood vessel next to her eye ticked.

"Are you all right?"

"Sorry. We deal with death a lot here. Don't expect to read grief on me the same way you would another." She met Joanna's eyes. "I know it's odd. He was my baby boy." The blood vessel pulsed more quickly, and her lips tightened. Her voice dropped to a whisper. "I swear I saw him last night."

"Before the pageant."

"No. After. Before the police called."

Joanna lowered her voice, as well. "You're under a lot of strain."

"Looking in the back door, right there." Adele turned to the kitchen door with its gingham curtain. "In drag, no less. A long gold dress. Isn't that funny? But he was dead the whole time."

The Halston. A shiver rippled down Joanna's arms.

"The police called not five minutes later." Her voice was flat, as if she were talking about seeing a neighbor pick up the paper, not about her own son. Her features, ropy with tension, belied her voice.

What was VC's brother's name? "Barry is here, of course, but do you have anyone else to stay with you for a few days?"

"You mean a husband? No husband. I kicked the boys' father out a long time ago." The pulse at her temple began to slow. "No. I've got lots of work to keep me busy. We'll be fine." She picked up the silk hibiscus and caressed its petals.

Sure, Adele had seen a lot of death, but not her own son's. Her world was going to be a blender of emotion for quite a while. "Bo was a special guy. I'm going to miss him."

Adele looked at her, eager for her words. "Yes."

"He was beautiful, of course." No doubt about where he got his looks. "But sensitive, too. I'm getting married on Sunday, and he always asked me how it was going. If I looked the slightest bit tired, he wanted to know what was wrong. He was kind."

Not two weeks after having met Bo, he'd brought a box of light bulbs to Tallulah's Closet. "These are soft light bulbs," he'd said. "We order them by the case for the funeral home—they give skin a lifelike glow, you know what I mean? I'll help you swap them out."

"Very kind," Bo's mother said. "He convinced us to adopt Buffy, here." The dog raised his head. "I didn't want to, didn't think we needed a dog to take care of on top of everything else. Buffy had belonged to an older woman who'd died. Her son brought him in when he made arrangements for his mother's care. Said Buffy was going to the pound." The dog rolled over, and she scratched him between the ears. "As always, Bo was right."

A bit of sun edged in the kitchen window. Concentrated by steely clouds, it left bright patches on the toaster and stainless steel refrigerator.

"Maybe I'd better go, leave you to get back to business." Joanna buttoned her jacket.

Adele pushed herself away from the table. "Not everyone likes a black man who dresses like a girl."

Joanna couldn't argue with that. But VC wasn't the only African-American performer at Marquise's. "You think his death might have been racially motivated?"

"Maybe. Maybe it was more personal." Adele strode out of the kitchen and into the hall running the length of the house's basement. "Come on."

Curious, Joanna followed her down the carpeted hall dimly lit by bronze sconces. "Where are we going?"

Adele opened a door. "My son's room."

"Bo's room." What was this about?

"Yes. That's what I said."

The room held a double bed, neatly made, a dresser, nightstand,

and that was it. It wasn't austere, but neither were its gray duvet and framed landscape brimming with character. Given Bo's personality, Joanna was surprised not to see some touch of flamboyance.

Adele moved to Bo's bedside table and pulled out its top drawer. Joanna hung back. "What are you looking for?"

"I don't know. Anything that's none of the police's business."

Joanna watched her rummage through its contents. Apparently nothing there interested her, because she opened the cupboard door below it and crouched to look inside. What was this with going through his things? Joanna had wanted to pass along the silk flower, offer her condolences. She hadn't expected to rifle through his bedroom.

"Come on," Adele said as if she'd read Joanna's mind. "Get busy. We've got to look through his stuff before the police get here."

"Why?" Despite her words, she'd already opened VC's closet. She'd always been nosy. Around a clothes closet, she was helpless.

"It's not what they'll find. It's what they'll find and not tell us. Besides, my son's personal life is none of their business." She stopped and fastened Joanna with her stare. "No one will pass judgement on my boy. You cared about him, too. Help me."

If Detective Crisp found out that she and a homicide victim's mother were rifling through the victim's belongings before the police had a chance to investigate, he'd have her scalp. Although it served him right for the hash he'd made of the investigation last night. "Are you sure this is a good idea?"

"I'm going to do it whether you're here to help or not." She pulled a box of tissues from a dresser drawer.

You couldn't really call VC's things evidence, Joanna reasoned. VC was the victim, not the murderer. Besides, curiosity was burning her up. She turned to the closet.

The closet, like the rest of the room, was meticulously ordered. Pressed trousers hung at regular intervals from wooden hangers. Next to them was a row of starched shirts with French cuffs. She'd sold VC cufflinks, she remembered, including a Depression-era opal set he'd loved. These must be what he wore to work in the funeral home. On the other side of the rack were his casual clothes: folded jeans, tee shirts, light sweaters in stacked crates. Other than a pearl white leather women's jacket that might pass as a man's, the closet held no drag costumes.

"Where did he keep his gowns?"

"Down the hall." Adele moved to VC's desk. "We'll look there next."

A few minutes later, apparently satisfied that Bo's room would stand up to police scrutiny, she led Joanna two doors down the hall. Adele pushed open the door. Ah, now this was more like it. A dinner mint-green love seat with a gold-framed mirror above it made a seating area in front of the closet, to the right of the door. On the wall between was a Lucite vanity with a mirror with etched flowers. Rose pink throw rugs covered the wood floor.

"Gorgeous," Joanna said. "It's like a set for a Fred Astaire and Ginger Rogers movie."

"He would have appreciated that," Adele said. "You take the racks, and I'll search the dresser. We're looking for personal notes, a diary, anything like that." She swung to Joanna. "If you find anything, hand it here. You understand."

"Got it." In other words, no peeking.

VC didn't have many gowns, but those she had were pure vintage goodness. Given her narrow physique, she'd wisely stuck to the mod shapes of the mid-1960s, the stretchy fit of the disco era, and the body-conscious 1980s. Joanna touched the pouf skirt of what looked to be a Christian Lacroix cocktail dress. She peeled open its bodice to look at the label. Yes, a genuine Lacroix. Amazing.

The black wool jersey dress next to it hung limply. Joanna knew that some of the best-fitting dresses look the worst on the hanger. She took a moment to spread it between her hands. Its sleeves were loose at the upper arm, then tightened through the forearm, and the neckline, modest in the front, plummeted in the back. If Joanna was right, this was an Alaïa with his signature butterfly sleeves. The label confirmed it. No wonder Bo went wild for the Halston. He had an unerring eye for quality.

"Where did Bo get these dresses? I sold him a few, but nothing as spectacular as these."

Adele knelt next to a pile of stockings and slips. "He was enterprising, my Bo. We tend to get higher end clients here. When he saw someone well turned out at a service, they talked."

Joanna reverently returned the Alaïa to the rack. "They're gorgeous."

"You should have them."

"What?"

Adele rose and touched Joanna's shoulder. "Once everything is settled, you should have Bo's gowns. He would have wanted it that way. You appreciate them. You'll make sure they find good homes."

"Oh, Adele. I couldn't...." Oh, yes, she could.

"Please."

When Joanna could speak, she whispered, "Thank you."

"Now, keep looking. I think that cape has pockets."

A man's voice jolted Joanna from her search. "What are you doing?" said VC's brother.

From where Joanna stood next to the door, she couldn't see to the hall. Barry moved to just inside the door. Joanna expected Adele, with her usual cool, to tell him to get lost—in sweeter words, of course.

But Adele froze. All at once she appeared pleasant, indifferent, like when Joanna first met her upstairs. Someone must be with Barry. A stranger.

"Mom…."

"Joanna," Adele said, uncertainty in her voice. She slowly rose to standing and slipped the dressing table drawer closed behind her.

Joanna joined Adele to better see out the door. She cursed under her breath.

Barry stepped aside. "Mom, this is Detective Crisp."

Chapter 5

Later that day, Joanna was straightening the dressing room at Tallulah's Closet when the phone rang.

"Hello?" Joanna's heart dropped. It was the Police Bureau. She hadn't wanted to install caller ID, but after some threatening calls the year before, Paul had convinced her it would be wise. She'd compromised by keeping her old rotary phone and finding a caller ID box at Goodwill. Two, in fact, so she'd have a backup.

"I need to see you," Detective Crisp said. "Right away."

Joanna swallowed. At the funeral home, he'd let her go with only a warning glance. She should have known she wouldn't get off that easily. "Now isn't the best time, I —"

"I said right away."

She bit her lip. "Okay. When will you be here?"

"I need to see you here, at the station. Within the next hour." He hung up without waiting for her reply.

Joanna slowly replaced the phone's receiver. Apple was helping a customer. She shot a glance back to Joanna before lifting the Priscilla of Boston gown Joanna had rejected that morning. "I knew from the second I saw this dress that it would be perfect for a wedding," she said, her back purposefully to Joanna.

"Oh, look." The customer lifted the dress's skirt, and the taffeta rustled softly. "It's like a princess's gown. Do you think it will fit?"

It would fit perfectly, Joanna thought. After years of running a vintage clothing shop, she could tell at a glance whether a dress needed half an inch more in the back or was made for a shorter-waisted woman.

"The only way to tell is to try it on," Apple replied. Apple was as good a judge of fit as she, but she was also a good saleswoman. Getting a customer to see a dress on her body was half the sale.

The customer took it to the dressing room.

Apple lifted an eyebrow to Joanna in a "satisfied?" motion. One less wedding dress option.

"I have to go downtown." Joanna lowered her voice. "To see Crisp."

"About this morning."

Joanna nodded. "I know you're supposed to leave at three, but can Gavin—" Apple's husband "—get dinner on his own?"

Apple turned away. "He'll be fine."

This again, Joanna thought. Something was going on. But whatever it was, it would have to wait. She shrugged on a green and red Pendleton 49ers jacket to go with her tartan skirt—she'd recently discovered she loved mixing plaids—and grabbed her purse, today a lipstick red 1960s Cashin Carry tote.

Crisp met her at the Police Bureau's reception area.

"Let's go to my desk," he said, not bothering with a greeting.

Joanna followed. Could she be charged with interfering in a homicide investigation? It's not as if she and Adele had found anything. She wished she'd paid more attention to criminal law in law school, but she'd dropped out partway through and pretty much cleansed her mind of anything having to do with torts and statutes.

They arrived at a cubicle festooned with crepe paper and balloons.

The cubicle was surprisingly impersonal, except for a framed photograph facing Crisp. Probably his wife. Joanna wished she could see it.

"Your birthday?" she asked. Maybe he'd be easier-going with cake in his system.

"Nope. I'm retiring," Crisp said. "They're throwing me a little party this week."

"Hey, Crisp," a uniformed policewoman said as she passed by. Crisp saluted in return.

Detective Foster Crisp was older, Joanna knew that, but she hadn't considered that he was nearing retirement. "Right away?"

"I'll be around a few weeks," he said. "Hopefully long enough to see this case put to bed. The judge will call me back if it goes to trial." He waved toward an office chair across his desk. "Have a seat."

She continued to stand. A stalling technique. "Any plans after retirement?"

"Sit," he repeated.

Reluctantly, she took the chair. The words tumbled out of her mouth. "It wasn't what it looked like."

"What?"

"At the funeral home. It wasn't what it looked like. VC's mother and I weren't disturbing evidence—"

"Then what were you doing?" His chair protested as Crisp leaned back.

"We were looking for things. Adele was afraid VC had a diary or something, and she wanted to find it—"

"Before we did?"

"She thought it might have, well, personal things in it."

"Doesn't matter. There was no diary—at least, nothing we found." He flipped through papers in his inbox while he talked.

"So, you didn't call me in here to bawl me out?"

"I should. You know better than that. Want a cup of coffee?"

"No, thank you." If he wasn't going to get on her case about searching VC's bedroom, what did he want? He'd offered her coffee. That was a good sign.

He tossed the papers back into the inbox. "That is, I won't make trouble for you if you give me some help."

"My help." This ought to be good. He'd gone out of his way to reject her help in the past.

"How well do you know those female impersonators?"

She half-smiled. "You can call them drag queens. It's fine. I knew VC because I helped her find clothes, and a few of the other girls stop by Tallulah's Closet sometimes. You know Marquise, right?"

He nodded. "Marquise's been around for fifty years. He and the department go way back."

"Why? They're not doing anything illegal, are they?"

"No. That's not why I asked you here."

"What do you need to know?"

Crisp crossed his cowboy boot-clad feet on the desk. "First let's start with the female impers—I mean drag queens. Can you tell me a little about how they work?"

"It's pretty obvious, Crisp. They dress up like women and entertain."

"No, I mean, the pronouns and all that. You call Vintage Chablis a 'she,' but Marquise is a 'he.'"

"In general, when someone is in drag as a woman, you refer to her as a 'she.' Marquise is so famous for his alter ego that most people call him Marquise, even in his street clothes. But when he's in drag, you say 'she.'"

"What about the names? Some of them have the same last name, but they're not related."

"When some men learn drag, they take on the family name of the person who inducted them into the life. Sometimes that means the same last name. Sometimes the family is named after a theme."

"A family, huh? What about Vintage Chablis?"

"Her family is named after jug wine. Their matriarch is Chianti Riserva." Joanna had been appalled the first time she'd heard "vintage" and "chablis" together. You don't want to drink most old chablis.

Crisp pulled his feet from his desk and sat up. "Here's the thing. They won't talk to us. No matter what we asked last night, they couldn't remember or didn't notice a thing."

"I'm not surprised, not with how you questioned them. You weren't respectful."

"I understood from what you said that Vintage Chablis — "

"We called her VC for short. Or, if you're uncomfortable, you can just say Bo."

"Let's just use the name on the birth certificate. You told me that Bo and another of the performers, Caramella, had some kind of dispute."

"Yes. I don't know any more about it than that, though."

"And no one will tell us any more, either," Crisp said.

"They said you guys have been picking on them. Did you check into the police cars Marquise told me were hanging around?"

"I did. It was part of another investigation. They were acting on a tip. Nothing came of it."

"What kind of tip required you to hassle the performers?"

"It's complicated, but the gist is that Portland is getting a reputation for being somewhere big operators come, then disappear. We were following one suspect, and he went into Marquise's."

"That could simply have been chance. Maybe he wanted to see

a show."

"He's one of the West Coast's biggest heroin distributors. He's known more for nightclubs and thousand-dollar champagne than ratty drag clubs. Look, I can't tell you more, and it doesn't matter since we've moved on."

Joanna folded her arms in front of her chest. "What have you got against drag queens, Crisp? You were unusually rude last night, and there you go calling Marquise's 'ratty.' What gives?"

The detective met her stare. "I don't know what you're talking about. Anyway, that's not why you're here. I want you to talk to some of the drag queens and see if you can find out anything about Bo Milton's fight with the other performer."

"Caramella, you mean?"

He nodded.

"Are you going to deputize me? Give me a badge?"

Crisp cracked a smile. "Don't you think we make a team already, with your plaid and my western wear?"

Joanna had to admit he was right. All she needed was a pony. "Seriously, though. I'm not a detective."

"You're not going to gather evidence. You'll be an informer. If you learn anything concrete, leave it alone. We'll follow up."

"I suppose I could ask Alexis. I'd feel a little uncomfortable about lying about it, though."

Crisp tossed his pen into the inbox. "Come on, Joanna. I found you snooping around this morning in Bo's bedroom. Don't tell me you're not dying to get more involved."

He was right, of course. "Fine. I guess I can ask a few questions. There's no guarantee she'll tell me anything."

"I'm sure you can be persuasive if you put your mind to it. Gossip.

You know, 'girl talk.'"

"Smirking doesn't suit you, Crisp."

"Just do a little speculating together. Someone must know why they were fighting."

Joanna settled back. It wouldn't be too hard to take Alexis out for a drink. The subject of VC's murder would come up naturally. Alexis had said she didn't know anything, but maybe with some gentle probing she'd remember something useful. "It might help if I knew what direction the case was taking. You know, have something to start the conversation."

"All right. I'll tell you what we know, but it isn't much. Between the medical examiner and the crime scene team, we know Bo was shot point-blank, likely with a larger caliber handgun. Nothing else would do that kind of damage. Ballistics is working on the details now."

A wave of nausea washed over Joanna. She breathed shallowly until it passed. Of course VC's face was gone. It had been blown away.

"You okay?"

"Yeah. Go on." Crisp wasn't telling her everything. She could tell by how he looked to the side as he spoke. "What else?"

"There is one more curious aspect, but it doesn't have to do with what I've asked you to do."

"Tell me. You can't ask me to collect information, then keep things from me."

Crisp met her gaze. "All right. You won't pass out on me?"

"I'm fine now. Tell me."

"It's the angle we found the body. Bo was face down, feet toward the wall before you turned him over."

Now she remembered. The gun must have been pointed toward the basement's interior and not toward the wall. "He could have stumbled a few steps and fallen, right?"

"It's more likely that the force of the gunshot pushed him in that direction, but it's unusual."

Two uniformed cops, probably rookies, waved as they passed. "Should we get some arthritis meds to go with that cake, Crisp?"

"Real funny," Crisp said.

Cake. Shoot. She'd have to get someone to make a cake for the wedding now that the caterer had dropped out. Later.

Crisp straightened. "Anyway, that's all we know. We got nothing out of the performers. The basement is closed off right now."

"So, no show tonight."

"Marquise said they wouldn't have held one, anyway."

"Yes." In a way, he was a combination of a large family's mother and a small community's mayor. He set the tone. They would mourn and support each other.

"Things are moving quickly." Crisp stood, indicating that their meeting was over. "The sooner you can get back to me, the better."

Chapter 6

Joanna would be happy never to live another day like the past twenty-four hours. The Fille Fantastique pageant, VC's death, meeting her family, searching VC's room and getting caught, then having Crisp actually ask her to help with the case. Then, having the wedding caterer back out. And she still had to find a dress. It was too much.

Thank goodness she was coming home.

"Hi, Jo," Paul said as she shut the front door behind her. The aroma of something onion-like—leeks?—reached her. Better yet, Paul was there. Home had always been her hideout, her safe place. Letting Paul in had been one of her better decisions.

"What are you making?" Joanna stopped at the kitchen table. A deadbolt lock set sat on a piece of newspaper next to a vase of peonies. "And what's this?"

"Dinner is risotto with spinach and leeks from the garden. Should be ready soon." He set down the wooden spoon and pulled her in, his chin resting on her head. "I picked up an old deadbolt at the job site today. That's your next lock picking lesson. It's time to move up from padlocks."

She wrapped her arms around his back. Gemma, Paul's German shepherd mix, nosed over to say hi.

"How was Crisp?" Paul asked.

She'd filled him in earlier on her visit to the funeral home and had left a message that she was headed to the Police Bureau. Reluctantly, she pulled away. "He wants me to see what I can find out about the fight between VC and Caramella. He blew it last night. None of the queens will talk to him."

"What does he want you to do?" A year ago, Paul would have pulled out all the stops to keep her from having anything to do with a murder investigation. Since then, he'd learned that one condition of being with her was to give her space. He'd even relaxed about his own past breaking into houses for his uncle to the point that he was willing to teach her how to pick locks. "For fun, that's it," he'd warned her.

"Talk to Alexis Campbell Starr, see if she has any insight. You're not worried, are you?"

"No. Crisp wouldn't put you on anything dangerous. At least, he'd better not." He tipped up her chin. "You have that look."

"Whatever it is, it isn't as good as your look." She pointed at his apron, one of hers in a mid-century print of poodles playing bridge. "Don't forget about the risotto."

"Keep talking." He picked up the spoon.

"I have to go out tonight, if Alexis will see me."

They looked at each other, Joanna waiting for Paul's reaction. "Better make your call," he said at last.

She went to the living room and set the phone on her lap. Hopefully, Alexis would pick up. So many people texted these days that getting anyone by voice was rare. Still, she didn't see a cell phone in her future. The sound quality wasn't as good, for one thing. And it didn't have that satisfying heft.

Alexis did answer, and she jumped at the chance to get a drink.

With that night's show at Marquise's cancelled, she was at loose ends. They arranged to meet at the bar directly behind Marquise's, where most of the performers went after shows.

"It's on," she told Paul. "I won't be out late." Pepper, her black cat, leapt to the couch next to her and dipped his head under her hand.

"You need to eat, though. Aunt Vanderburgh says so," came Paul's voice from the kitchen.

She glanced at the thrift store portrait she'd named Aunt Vanderburgh. She'd used Auntie V as a sounding board many times, but less often now that Paul lived with her. As far as she knew, Paul didn't talk to the portrait, but the portrait apparently used him to relay messages from time to time.

She returned to the kitchen and leaned against the refrigerator. "We have an hour and a half before I have to be there." Gemma moved to lie over her feet. "You're getting to be a fabulous cook."

"I like it." He dropped a handful of chopped parsley into the risotto.

"How would you feel about catering the wedding?"

Paul turned off the heat and put a lid on the risotto. "That doesn't mean what I think, does it?"

Joanna folded her arms over her chest.

"Oh, no," he said. "The caterer bailed?"

"Family emergency."

"I'm fine with a trip to the courthouse, remember. Or a wedding with no deluxe meal. It's the marriage that counts, not the ceremony."

They agreed on that count. If she could have a marriage as solid as Apple and Gavin's, she'd be happy. They always seemed to have each other's back, be looking out for each other.

"I know," Joanna said. "Thank you. I want something we'll remember."

He shook his head. "Have you found a dress yet?"

"Apple found a gorgeous Eisenhower-era gown, in fact." Gorgeous for someone else, that is.

"Let me guess. It just wasn't right."

"Too formal. We sold it a few hours later, though. Doubled our income for the day. Don't worry, I'll find the right one."

"I don't care what you wear or what we eat, you know that."

Joanna slipped her foot out from under the dog and put an arm around Paul's waist.

"As long as you show up, that's all I care," he said.

"Oh, I'll be there."

*
**

Alexis—Austin, tonight—stood outside Imago Mundi smoking a cigarette. As Joanna approached, a couple walked past him, the wife ostentatiously waving the smoke away from her face. The cigarette was long and white between Austin's dark, coral-tipped fingers.

"Hi, honey," he said and kissed Joanna on both cheeks. "Mind if we stay outside a minute while I finish this?"

"That's fine." The spring night was mild, if damp, drawing the odor of urine from the alley. Old Town was a motley collection of nineteenth-century buildings, a few nightclubs, and most of the city's homeless shelters, with a sprinkling of some of the more pioneering design and architecture offices. On weekends, the streets teemed with suburban partiers. On a Monday night, like tonight, it was mostly locals stopping for a beer after work and tossing coins into the boxes set out by transients settled into doorways for the night.

Austin turned his face toward the streetlight just as it came on. His skin had an almost iridescent smoothness about it. He was about as tall as VC, but rounder, giving his face a look of innocence that his attitude more than made up for. He wore a black leather baseball cap studded with rhinestones.

"Broadway, baby," he said, nodding toward the streetlight. "The lights can't help but shine on me." He tossed the cigarette butt in the gutter. "Let's get a drink."

A low murmur of conversation filled Imago Mundi. Austin waved at the bartender, and they settled into a high-backed booth against an exposed brick wall.

"I've never been here," Joanna said.

"This place is all about maps. Imago Mundi. It's some kind of map. Look." He picked up a plastic-sheathed menu, its front a replica of a medieval map.

A waiter, eyes on another couple hesitating at the door, took their order. Joanna requested her usual martini, and Austin took a vodka soda. "I'll give you the service industry discount," the waiter said as he collected their menus.

"Bring us some stuffed mushrooms, too," Austin added.

"A discount? Not bad," Joanna said.

"When the owner was renovating, he made all sorts of trouble for Marquise. Broke a pipe and flooded the back of the basement. Even had to shore up the joists between the buildings. They share a back wall. That"—Austin pointed toward the restaurant's rear—"is the other side of the stage at Marquise's."

"So he's giving you a discount for the trouble."

"Plus, we're regulars."

The waiter set their drinks on napkins, also printed with maps. "Food will be up in a minute."

"I like the chicken fingers at C.C.'s better, but VC was a fan of the stuffed mushrooms here. It seems right to have them tonight."

They fell silent a moment. "It's awful," Joanna whispered. Just a day before, just yards away, VC was killed. "At least it was sudden. She couldn't have felt anything."

Austin ran a finger down the condensation on his glass. "Marquise is hiring a guard to watch the basement entrance during show hours. I think he feels responsible."

"A good idea, even if it's really not his fault."

"The police are questioning Roger pretty hard, too."

"Roger?"

"The cook. Roger Bing. He probably feels as bad as Marquise does. Roger's devoted to him. Marquise found him on the streets years ago and gave him a job cleaning up after the show. Now he's in charge of food. Blames himself for letting the gunman through."

"This is no time for blame. Or guilt," Joanna said. At last, she tasted the martini. Nice and dry. Not bad.

"I'm going to miss her," Austin said, his eyes bright with tears. He looked down at his drink.

"Me, too. VC was a one-of-a-kind." Her throat tightened. "I met her family this morning. I had one of VC's silk flowers, so I dropped it by. Thought they'd want it. Have you met her mother?"

"Adele? Yes." Austin seemed glad for the distraction. "Talk about beautiful. She was a model for *Ebony*, you know."

"I'm not surprised," Joanna said, remembering Adele's almost Egyptian eyes. Model to funeral home director. Not your usual career path. "Has the funeral home been in the family for long?"

"Adele picked it up after Bo's dad left. She sank her earnings into it, got certified as a funeral director, and voilà. She runs it, with her sons' help."

Joanna remembered Adele's strangely calm reaction to her son's death, and then her abrupt, almost frenzied searching of his room.

"Bo played the organ at services, too. He was good," Austin said, lapsing to VC's birth name.

"You two were friends, then."

"I'd call him a friend. Sure. We didn't see each other much except after shows, though. Bo kept to himself. He was private."

Joanna returned her glass to the map-printed napkin. Time to get down to business. "I keep thinking about VC and Caramella's fight. They must have had some reason for going at each other like that."

"Well, well," a hearty voice interrupted them. The voice quieted. "I was so sorry to hear about the accident next door."

"Joanna, this is Lewis Custard," Austin said. "He owns the place. Lewis, meet Joanna."

Lewis Custard. She couldn't help but think of a board game and "in the billiards room with the lead pipe." He looked the part, too, with his curly red beard trimmed to a point, generous figure, and wire-rimmed glasses.

Joanna traded glances with Austin. "I'm afraid it was worse than an accident."

"I saw the police cars and the ambulance. It wasn't Marquise, was it? Heart trouble?" Reacting to Joanna and Austin's expressions, he straightened. "Sorry. I used to be a physician."

"No. No, I'm afraid it was VC. She was killed."

The man's face blanched beneath his beard. "VC. She was so young. I can't believe it." The owner turned to a passing waiter. "This table's check is on the house." Then, back to Austin and Joanna. "What happened?"

Austin recapped the pageant and its horrible ending. "We're having a memorial service the day after tomorrow. Marquise will be by to invite you, I'm sure."

"I'll bring food. Maybe a few platters of stuffed mushrooms. VC always liked them." Lewis swallowed a few times, his head bobbing like an ostrich's. "This neighborhood isn't safe. I've got a good security system, but you can't be too careful."

Joanna toyed with a stuffed mushroom. Its bread crumb topping was crisp without being greasy, and fresh parsley, chopped fine, topped it. A thought occurred to her. "You don't cater, do you?" Asking about food for a wedding right after talking about a murder seemed insensitive. Then again, it wouldn't hurt to change the subject, and she needed to pull conversation back to Caramella somehow.

"Small jobs. Planning something?"

"I'm getting married on Sunday, and the caterer pulled out. A small event, only about twenty-five of us. We'll need lunch. Nothing fancy. I know it's last minute."

Lewis Custard slipped a business card from his pocket. "Give me a call tomorrow, and we can talk." He stepped back. "Again, I'm so sorry to hear about VC. Maybe I'll drop by and tell Marquise about my security outfit. Couldn't hurt. VC." He shook his head and moved off.

Austin pulled the tiny straw from his glass. "I almost expect to see VC come in any moment. This afternoon, I found an old hairpiece I thought would look great on her, then I remembered."

"I know the feeling." Joanna looked down the long bar and the row of booths facing it, to the pool of tables in the restaurant's depths. "Austin, something was going on between her and Caramella. Someone killed VC, and I don't think it was random."

"Caramella would never shoot her."

"She put pins in VC's wigs."

"And she swapped out her shoes for smaller ones, and loosened her side seams so they'd give out while she was on stage. Just a little sabotage. And maybe the occasional insult."

"Do you know what all that was about?"

Austin jingled the ice cubes in his nearly empty glass. "Nope. Like I told you, no one did."

"You don't have any idea at all?"

"Nothing."

"Or maybe there was some kind of romantic dispute? Maybe they both went after the same guy."

Austin shook his head. "That's the strange thing. Neither one of them was big on dating. Caramella never talked about anyone since I've known her."

This was going nowhere fast. "Tell me about her."

He leaned back. "His name is Lorenzo Perez. He's a contractor—his family has a construction business doing odd jobs. Perez's Handy Helpers. I don't think they're keen on his other life. That's about all I can tell you."

Frustrating. "Except that he had it in for VC." Lorenzo Perez. She made a mental note.

"Yeah." Austin's gaze took in the bar crowd. "They had a whopper of a fight here last week, in fact."

Joanna's attention sharpened. "About what?"

"Who knows? They yelled at each other, called each other names, and VC threw a vodka cranberry at Caramella. The bartender had to break them up."

"But no accusations?"

He shook his head. "Nothing. Just a lot of fighting." He looked her in the eyes. "Look, Jo. I know you feel responsible somehow since you found her, but don't let it get to you." He nodded at the half-full martini glass. "Drink up."

Chapter 1

The next morning, Joanna rearranged the dresses at Tallulah's Closet by color. She hadn't expected to work this morning, but Apple had called in sick. It was for the best. Joanna needed to keep busy.

She pondered her progress — or lack of it — figuring out the core of Caramella and VC's dispute. The conflict with Caramella might well be at the center of VC's death. What else could it be? VC was popular. Her family loved her. Here, Joanna paused, a red Thierry Mugler suit in hand. At least, her mother did. Perhaps VC's brother wasn't on board with her drag life, but disapproval was hardly a reason for murder. The other queens adored VC. She didn't seem to have problems at work, either at the funeral home or Marquise's. Caramella was the open question. Alexis wasn't a help. Whom could she talk to next?

She needed a plan. Maybe there would be more to learn at the memorial service, but she couldn't count on it. If Alexis didn't know what had sparked the animosity between VC and Caramella, Joanna didn't know who else would.

Joanna slipped the Mugler suit on the rack, and, with a crash, the rod ripped away from the wall, dumping six feet of dresses, suits, and coats on the carpet.

She stifled a moan and stood, hands on hips, looking at the pile of fabric, while Herb Alpert cheerfully tootled "The Spanish Bull" from the stereo. That's it. She'd have to call Paul and see if he could fix it. He was helping restore a Victorian staircase in an old timber baron's mansion on the west side, but he might be able to get to it tonight, after the store closed.

She began piling dresses on the red bench in the center of the store, then stopped. Paul wasn't the only handy guy in town. She didn't have to quiz the town's drag queens to find out more about VC and Caramella. She could go straight to Caramella herself.

From under the tiki bar, Joanna pulled a dog-eared phone book. It was getting harder to find them, thanks to everyone's reliance on the internet. This directory was a few years old, but with any luck Caramella's firm would be listed. What did Austin say it was called? Perez something. Bingo. There it was, Perez's Handy Helpers.

She dialed. A busy-sounding voice answered.

"Your ad says you make emergency visits. I have an emergency," she said.

"What ad?"

"Your ad in the phone book."

A pause. "That has to be years old. Don't even try to use the coupon."

"I don't care about the coupon. I need one of your handy helpers."

The door's bell jangled as a customer entered, shaking an umbrella. She moved slowly, as if lifting her feet was an effort. The customer glanced at the pile of clothes on the bench on her way to the black cocktail dresses. Joanna waved and raised a finger to indicate she'd be with her in a moment.

"It's an emergency?"

"I own a vintage clothing shop, and one of my clothing rods just fell down. Could you come fix it? I'm hoping you'll send Lorenzo.

I hear he's great."

"Lorenzo's not working today. Besides, our schedule's full right now. I could get someone there tomorrow late morning at the earliest."

"I'd really like Lorenzo. Is there any way you could convince him to come? Maybe with double pay?" She crossed her fingers and wondered if Crisp would chip in.

"I don't know—"

"Please," she said. She knew she sounded mournful, and it didn't come from the broken rack. "It would mean so much to me."

She heard a long exhale. "Double pay, you say? Let me look." A moment passed before the voice came back on the line. "Ernesto might have the time at about three."

"Needs to be Lorenzo. He's the only one I trust."

He sighed. "I'll check. What's your address?"

Joanna replaced the receiver and smiled at the customer. "Is there anything in particular you're looking for?"

The woman slumped toward a display of Lucite box purses. "I don't know."

"A special event?" The customer wore mall clothes, and right now they were wrinkled and haphazardly matched. She probably didn't wear vintage often. "Or maybe you just want to look around."

"I need something to wear to my sister's wedding."

Joanna turned to a circular rack with patterned dresses. She had a few good candidates here that would save her from having to dig through the dresses heaped on the bench. The woman looked to be about an eight, and on the short side. The sprigged 1940s rayon dress would be lovely on her and perfect for a wedding.

"How about this?" Joanna said. "The asymmetrical neckline and peplum are super flattering. Are you a bridesmaid?"

"Nope." The woman turned back to the black cocktail dresses. "I want one of these."

Black? For a wedding? The customer was always right. "An evening wedding, then."

"Nope."

Joanna forced a smile and flipped through the black dresses. "Let's see. Do you have an idea on style?"

"Lots of boob."

What kind of wedding was this? "You mean, like this?" Joanna pulled a disco-era dress from the rack. It was slit up the leg and wrapped at the chest in a low V neck. Long strings of polyester welt studded with rhinestones made its belt. It had never been one of Joanna's favorites, but Apple had insisted they buy it. She'd said some teenager would jump on it for the prom.

But there was no way it was appropriate at a wedding. Joanna was returning it to the rack when the woman said, "Yeah. That one. Let me try that one."

"The dressing rooms are in the back. I'll look for a few others while you're in there."

In a trance, the woman moved toward the dressing rooms.

The bell at the door jangled again. This time it was Paul. Joanna lit up. "I thought you were working on the staircase today."

"I had to come back to pick up a few things. Thought I'd stop by and see how you're doing."

"Better now that you're here." It was true. Seeing him infused her with warmth.

Paul picked up an astrakhan-trimmed suit from the pile of clothes on the bench. "What happened here?"

"I don't know. The rack came right off the wall."

"Let me fix it. I have some tools in the truck."

"No," Joanna said. "I already called someone."

"Why? You know it would only take me a second to shore this up."

The doorbell rang yet again, and Lorenzo Perez entered carrying a toolbox. If Joanna hadn't known he might be stopping by, she wouldn't have recognized him. His dirty tee shirt and jeans were worlds away from Caramella's flashy, but meticulous, outfits. He looked like he'd just rolled out of bed. "You need something fixed?" His eyes narrowed. "It's you. VC's friend."

"What a coincidence," Joanna said with false cheer.

"You're paying double time, right?"

Paul looked from Lorenzo to Joanna. "Double time? I told you I can fix this."

The dressing room curtains rustled from the rear of the store. The woman emerged, wrapped in curvaceous black polyester. She burst into wracking sobs.

Good grief. Joanna turned to her. "What's wrong?"

"Why are there men here?"

"One of them's my boyfriend—"

The woman's sobs jumped a few decibels.

"And the other's here to fix the clothing rack."

"I can fix the rack," Paul said again, looking at Lorenzo.

"Make them go away. I'm going back in the dressing room, and I'm not coming out until they're gone." She ducked behind the curtain and yanked it shut hard enough that a ring popped off the panel.

What a mess. First, she had to get Paul out of here. Maybe the customer would calm down. She slipped her arm through Paul's. "We'll talk later," she whispered and kissed his cheek. "Thanks for stopping by."

"You're sure—"

"I'll be in touch."

He glanced at Lorenzo on his way out. "Double time? Really?"

Lorenzo set down his toolbox and marched to the dressing room. "Honey," he said.

"Go away," the woman said and sniffed loudly.

Joanna bit her lip. Should she send Lorenzo away? She wanted to talk to him about VC, but it was impossible with this customer. The customer's sobbing made up her mind. "I'm so sorry. I'll pay you for your time, but you'd better leave."

"What's she doing in there?" he asked.

"Trying on a dress for her sister's wedding." Why did he care?

Lorenzo waved Joanna away. He seemed less tired now, a little more alert. "Honey," he said again to the customer. "You still have that dress on?"

"Yes," came the reply through sniffles.

"Come out and show me."

"No."

Joanna leaned forward. "Really. You'd better leave."

Lorenzo ignored her. "I just want to check the fit on the back. I think you can use a little more drape."

Slowly, the woman emerged from behind the curtain. Tears stained her cheeks. Lorenzo handed her a fresh handkerchief. She turned her back, as he'd asked.

"That's what I thought." He pulled an inch of fabric from the back. "See? This style needs drape up top to balance the tight bottom."

The customer turned to face him. Her eyes were red, and mascara rimmed their edges. She wiped her eyes with the back of her hand. "Okay," she almost whispered.

Lorenzo pulled up the stool Joanna kept for trying on shoes. "Now what's a pretty girl like you doing wearing that skanky thing to a wedding?"

"I wouldn't call it skanky, exactly—" Joanna started.

The customer sniffed but didn't respond.

"So, it's like that, is it?" he said. "She went and got engaged to your man, am I right?"

"We were dating first. He said he loved me. Then she started seeing him behind my back…." Sobbing, the woman fell into his arms.

He patted her back. "Darling, congratulations. You've now officially got rid of that jerk. Dodged a bullet, I say."

"But it hurts so bad."

"You don't have to tell me about pain. I know about pain," he said. "I know about wanting to hurt someone because he hurt you. But we're going to fix that."

The woman leaned away. "How?"

"Revenge, honey."

Joanna sat up straighter. The Herb Alpert record had ended, but she didn't want to move away to change it.

"What do you mean?"

"He needs to be real sorry for what he did."

A chill prickled the back of Joanna's arms.

"We're going to make you look so good that you feel like a superstar," Lorenzo said. "Not a tramp. You're going to parade into that wedding with a 'la-di-da, screw you.'"

Paul appeared with his toolbox. Joanna reluctantly left Lorenzo and the customer to meet him by the door. "You came back. You, my friend, are stubborn."

"I've been thinking about it. I can fix the rack. There's no need to pay anyone."

Lorenzo was deep in discussion with the customer at the store's rear.

"That's Caramella, the queen who had it out for VC," she whispered. "I wanted to talk to her, see if I could dig up something for Crisp."

"Well, he's here now. How about if I fix the rack in the meantime?"

Paul couldn't help himself, Joanna knew. She glanced warily at the customer. "All right."

"Let's have some music," Lorenzo shouted. "Something upbeat. Girlfriend here needs a dress."

Joanna looked at Paul. He shrugged. "I have a disco favorites album. How about that?" she shouted back.

"Maybe some Gloria Gaynor?" he said. "A little, you know, 'I Will Survive'?"

"I'll play that first."

An hour later, the customer had left with a smile and two items—a red dress that hugged her curves without an R rating, and a pale pink dressing gown "for your alone time, your special time," as Lorenzo had put it. The clothing rack was fixed, and Paul had returned to the stairwell job.

Lorenzo stayed. He helped Joanna return the dresses to the rack and seemed in better spirits than he had when he'd come in. "You didn't ask me here to fix anything. Not with that man around."

"He wasn't here when you arrived," she said.

"This rack was just an excuse."

Joanna moved a blue dress so it was grouped with the other blue items in a spectrum from the cornflower blue of china plates to rich navy. She would simply come out with it. "It's about VC."

"Ah." Lorenzo handed her the last item, a red cotton shirtwaist dress.

"Do you have any idea why someone would have killed VC?"

Lorenzo examined Joanna. "We had a feud, and you wonder if I killed her. That's why I'm here." He stepped back. "That's why you called."

She didn't respond.

"You called me here, and you knew I'd bring a box of tools." His expression hardened to disgust. "I've got things in there that could kill you in seconds."

"What are you saying?" She wished Paul were still there. Or anyone else.

"I'm stronger than you. We're alone. It would be easy."

Joanna's breath quickened. It was all talk. Had to be. There was a jar of hatpins on the jewelry counter, but that was at least ten feet away.

"What's wrong? Cat got your tongue?" Lorenzo gazed out the window, a faraway look in his eyes. "Well, I got nothing to say, either."

He picked up his toolbox and left.

"Apple?" Joanna picked up the phone and carried it to the store's bench. "Feeling any better?"

"I'm all right," she said. "Have you found a wedding dress yet?"

"I will. I'm not worried." That was a lie. "Good news on the catering, though. The guy who owns Imago Mundi is going to do it. The food's not bad, either."

It was toward the end of the day, and judging from the crowd wandering past Tallulah's Closet, business at Dot's, the bar next door, was picking up. Sometimes a group of women would come in the store while their boyfriends drank beer next door, so Joanna stayed open through happy hour.

At last, Apple sounded more encouraged. "He can do a whole lunch for twenty-five people?"

"Said it was no problem. I'm meeting with him tomorrow."

"That's great news. I'm relieved."

"You and me both." Aside from the wedding gown, she was back on track. "Someone else called from the ad. They're going to drop a wedding dress by. This one sounds good. Mid-sixties, long, not as formal as the last one."

"There's barely time for alterations. I hope it fits."

Joanna hoped it fit, too, especially now that she didn't even have the Priscilla of Boston to fall back on. "You sound tired."

She sighed. "I am."

"Apple, what's wrong? You've been out of sorts for the past couple of weeks. You're not telling me something."

She laughed, a hollow laugh. "I'm fine. Just off my game. You know."

This was not like Apple. Normally she was the upbeat one, encouraging Joanna to get out more or drink some sort of tincture or herbal smoothie to boost her chi.

"You want me to bring you something? I suppose Gavin is taking care of that, though."

The phone was silent. The faint bass of a Roxy Music song vibrated through the wall Tallulah's Closet shared with Dot's Cafe.

"Apple?" Joanna prompted.

A vaguely familiar young woman in a navy business suit entered the store. It was rare to see women in suits these days, especially a blue one. The color gave her the unfortunate air of being in the Salvation Army. But instead of a tuba, she carried a leather attaché, which meant she wasn't the person who'd called with a wedding dress. Where did she know this woman from? Seeing Joanna on the phone, she half-heartedly examined a dropped-waist gold velvet flapper-style dress.

"You need your gown," Apple said. "The wedding is less than a week away. This is ridiculous. A woman who owns a dress shop ought to have something to wear to her own wedding."

"I'll find something." She willed this to be true. "Maybe this next dress will be the perfect one."

"You'd better hope so." Joanna opened her mouth to tell Apple she had a customer and would call her back, when Apple said, "Are you going to VC's service?"

"Definitely." Today's attempts to learn more about Caramella failed, but she was hoping the memorial service would offer opportunities. "I'm meeting with the caterer just before it. Do you think you'll be up to working, or should I close early?"

A long sigh reached Joanna's ears. "I'll be fine."

"You're sure?" Why was Apple being so secretive?

"I'm just a little under the weather, that's all."

"Let's touch base tomorrow. A customer just came in."

Hearing this, the suited woman approached the tiki bar. "Joanna Hayworth?"

Joanna replaced the receiver. "Yes. Are you looking for something special?" She'd already mentally selected a dark red wool suit from the 1950s with a nipped waist for the woman to try. With brown heels—luggage brown was terrific with a mid-century cranberry red—she'd rock the suited look. It was much better than that cheap blue thing she wore.

"I'm from the Morning Glory bed and breakfast. You rented it for your wedding."

Joanna smiled, but her intuition sounded warning bells. This woman wasn't here for a suit. "I thought I recognized you. How are things? I was planning to call tomorrow morning. We're changing caterers."

The woman toyed with business cards Joanna had set in a shell-shaped porcelain dish. "I wanted to come in person."

Joanna's heart sank. "Yes?"

"I'm afraid I have some bad news." From the woman's pleading eyes, the news was as hard on her as she anticipated it would be on Joanna. "A pipe upstairs broke and flooded the first floor. It'll be at least a week before the house is back to normal."

"The house doesn't have to be perfect. As long as there's room to eat and have the ceremony—"

"It's worse than dampness, I'm afraid. We pulled up the carpets, and there's dry rot all along the joists. The plumber thinks it's been leaking for years."

Joanna felt for a seat behind her. There had to be something they could do about the venue. "So, it's hopeless? You're sure?"

The woman clenched her hands. "I'm afraid so. I brought you back your deposit."

Five days until the ceremony. What was she going to do? "My wedding." The words came out in a tiny voice.

"I'm so, so sorry."

Chapter 8

The next afternoon, Joanna parked down the block from Marquise's. A handwritten sign posted on the door said that Marquise's would be closed that night for a "private event." People passing by might have thought it was a bachelorette or birthday party. Few would have suspected it was for a dead man.

She carried a long sheaf of star magnolia branches for the memorial service. She'd visited a florist, but the tulips and gladioli in plastic sleeves were soulless. She wanted something with VC's drama and charming imperfections, so she raided her own garden. The flowers would barely last the evening, but that was somehow fitting, too.

Joanna passed Marquise's and walked around the corner to Imago Mundi. Happy hour had just begun, and only a few people sat at the bar. Just two booths were taken. Maybe she'd be able to get in a word with the bartender, see if he had any ideas about Caramella and VC's fights.

Instead, Lewis Custard met her right away. "Joanna. Martini, nice and dry, with a twist. Did I remember right?" He slid his bulk onto the stool and patted the one next to his in an invitation to join him. He seemed to have taken pains to smooth his beard, and, like her, he wore black.

"If it's not too much trouble." She placed her clutch and flowers on the bar and took a stool.

"I take it you're going to VC's service, too," Lewis said.

"Yes." Joanna wore a simple 1940s crepe dress with three-quarter length sleeves and just a hint of shoulders. She'd chosen a matching cameo bracelet and necklace to go with it. VC would have liked them. "It seems odd to talk about a wedding right before a memorial service."

"Passages of life," Lewis said. "In some African tribes, when the head of a family dies, at his funeral ceremony a chosen brother attempts to impregnate the wife." At Joanna's startled twitch, he dipped his head. "I'm sorry. It's easier to spout anthropological trivia than deal with death."

"Did you know VC well?"

"No. Other than seeing her here, not at all, really. But I'm close to Marquise's community. I feel it." Lewis raised his hand, and the bartender, a thin man with bleached hair carefully combed to hide a receding hairline, stood at attention. "Joanna here would like a martini."

"Vodka or gin?" the bartender asked.

"Gin, if you please," he said sternly. Then, to Joanna, "I've told them to serve gin when someone orders a martini, but there are simply too many people who drink vodka. Infidels."

"I'm with you. There's no such thing as a vodka martini. Only vodka cocktails."

"I'm more of a Scotch man, but I respect that."

The martini appeared on the oak bar, and the bartender, without asking, set a low tumbler of brown liquid and ice in front of Lewis. "Cheers," Lewis said. "I only wish it could be a more joyous occasion."

"Maybe someone will try to knock up one of the queens tonight." Joanna raised the glass to her lips and sampled the gin's bite.

"Touché." Lewis slid from his seat. "Shall we take these upstairs? We can discuss the menu there, where it's more quiet."

"You live upstairs?"

"Just like a shopkeeper. Yes, I own the whole building. Bought it when I sold my medical practice."

Gingerly holding her cocktail, Joanna followed Lewis to the restaurant's rear, into the hall with the bathrooms. Lewis unlocked a door that could have been a utility closet, but which opened into a staircase.

"Alexis says a lot of the girls from Marquise's come to Imago Mundi."

"I give them the service industry discount. Local color. Patrons love it when they come in drag."

She calculated her next words. "The customers don't mind the attitude? I know the performers can get loud sometimes, especially if they're amped up after a show. I've heard VC and Caramella, for instance, used to get into it."

Lewis raised an eyebrow. "They did, at that."

He motioned for Joanna to climb the stairs ahead of him. The door at the top opened into a kitchen. "Come this way." He led her to the front of the building, where a living room ran the width of the apartment. A low seating area of white leather couches with a large, square coffee table filled the room's center. One wall was windows, showing the street's rain-blackened tree branches breaking into bud.

Joanna saw all this as normal for the apartment of a well-to-do bachelor. What was unusual were the framed maps covering the walls from floor to ceiling. The map across from her showed dragons rising from the sea.

The setting sun reflected in Lewis's glasses. "You notice my maps."

"They're beautiful."

"Mapmaking is an art, but a science, too. Sometimes you know the point of origin and the destination, but the rest is unknown. Filled by imagination. Like the real Imago Mundi."

"What you named your restaurant after. It means 'image of the world,' or something like that, doesn't it?"

"It was a stone tablet found in Babylonia. They guess it to be from five hundred years before the birth of Christ. It shows seven tiny islands with names like 'beyond the flight of the birds.' The in-between is blank."

"Like the facts of VC's death," Joanna couldn't help noting.

"Indeed. Horrible."

She took in another sweeping glance of the walls, colorful with wavy coastlines and imaginary oceans. "How did you get so interested in maps?"

"I have a lung condition and can't fly. A shame. I've always been fascinated by the rest of the world, ever since I was a child, forced to stay home from school. The maps have become a bit of an obsession, a way to see the world."

"Maybe that explains your interest in medicine. Your lung condition, that is."

He smiled. "Very observant." He picked up an auction catalog on the table and opened it to a marked page. "This is the next map I have my eye on."

Joanna choked a bit on her martini when she saw the expected value. The restaurant business must be more lucrative than she'd thought.

"It's a medieval French map of Africa. Stunning detail. Mapmaking is only now getting the attention it deserves as an art. It's about so much more than finding your way."

They were surrounded by a king's ransom in old maps. "Will the sunlight damage them?"

"Oh, no. Those are replicas. I keep the real maps under archival conditions in a special room, back there."

A thought occurred to Joanna. She leaned forward. "Could VC's death have to do with this? Maybe someone was trying to break in through Marquise's to get to the maps."

"It's happened before. An attempted robbery, that is. But coming through an adjacent building seems foolhardy, not to mention unnecessary."

Joanna relaxed into the couch again. "I suppose so. I just don't understand why VC was killed."

"I've thought about it, too, and admit I'm stumped." He lifted his glass to his lips, but the level of the Scotch remained constant. "You asked about Caramella earlier. You suspect her?"

"I saw Caramella and VC argue just before VC was killed. You would have a better idea of their relationship, having seen them downstairs."

He set his tumbler on the coffee table. "I'd call their arguments mostly playful. I didn't hear any real threat. If you asked me, I might even have thought it was a game. Could have been a mere publicity stunt."

"What sorts of things did they argue about?"

Lewis appeared to think it over. "I can't say it was about anything in particular, really. They simply insulted each other." He started to laugh but cut it short. "In clever ways, actually. But, no, I never heard accusations. You found her—VC—didn't you?"

Joanna nodded. "Found her" seemed inadequate. Thinking of Marquise and of VC's family at the funeral home, "turned worlds upside down" was more on target.

He pulled back his cuff and looked at his watch. "We'd better get on with choosing a lunch menu for you. The service is in half an hour."

She rested her now empty glass on the table. "I'm so glad you can do this at the last minute. We won't need anything fancy." Goodbye, salmon and pea shoot soup.

"What are the kitchen facilities like at your venue?"

"I'm not sure. Yet." She explained that they were looking for a new spot for the wedding. Her calls to other venues that morning had been unsuccessful, but a few months ago, Penny, the customer and friend who'd bought the Halston, had volunteered her riverside home for the ceremony. Joanna had left a message with her that morning. She crossed her fingers that it was still available. "Is a home kitchen a possibility?"

"We can make it work." Lewis examined her a moment. He pushed aside Imago Mundi's menu. "Certainly, we can do better than the bar food downstairs—good as it is, if I might add."

With hope, Joanna said, "The spring Chinook run has started. I might have a connection to some fresh fish."

"Perhaps with an asparagus soup? Or pea shoot? I see chive blossoms sprinkling the fillet."

This was going to work after all. Together, Lewis and Joanna planned a menu at least as good as the one the first caterer had offered.

If only gathering information for Crisp were as easily remedied as patching up her wedding. Well, Caramella would be at the service. Perhaps Joanna would have better luck tonight.

Chapter 6

Marquise met Lewis and Joanna at the door. As Joanna's eyes adjusted to the dark, she made out dozens of votive candles lighting the theater. Candles sat on the tiny tables between chairs. Candles lined the stage. Candles filled the nooks at the bar and at the window where orders came up from the kitchen. The room was a constellation fallen to earth.

Grief thickened in Joanna's throat and filled her eyes.

"Thank you," she whispered to Marquise. Not in drag, Marquise looked smaller, grayer. His eighty-plus years showed in his liver-spotted hands and loose skin beneath his eyes. Marquise's partner of many years, Foxy, sat nearby, his cane at his knee.

Lewis gave a shallow bow and walked toward the seats. Joanna lingered back.

"I'm so glad you could come, dear," Marquise said. "It'll be just us girls and a few friends, but we had to have our own ceremony before the official funeral."

"There will be a funeral, then?" Joanna asked. "I mean—" She didn't know what she meant. Of course there'd be a funeral. Bo grew up in a funeral home. He'd probably have a top-flight casket with a glitter blanket wrapping him.

"I called the family and asked if they'd like to come. I didn't expect them to say yes, and they didn't. His mother—such a beautiful woman, have you met her?"—Marquise paused long enough for Joanna to nod—"said the medical examiner wasn't ready to send her son home yet. The funeral is a few days away."

Joanna brushed his cheek with a kiss. "I'll find a seat."

From the few times she'd been at Marquise's with VC, she'd seen what a warm community it was. It took courage for a man to dress as a woman. Here, it was safe. No matter what the outside world said, here you could be yourself and as fabulous as you wanted. Marquise had spent more than fifty years fostering a multi-generational family of men, many of whom had been ostracized from their birth families. Joanna thought of Bo's brother, Barry. No doubt Marquise's had been a haven for VC.

Joanna took a seat a few rows back from the stage. The theater was half full, and most of the occupants were queens of varying ages who, unlike Marquise, had come in drag. Mourning drag, that is. While the girls wore black, and many had veils pinned to their wigs, their dresses tended toward the sequined and décolleté, and, to a one, they wore heels.

Summer Seasons, also in drag, slipped into the seat next to Joanna. "May I?" Summer favored lavender and the muted pinks of an English garden's border. They complemented her honey-blonde hair and sweet—well, mostly—personality.

"Please." Joanna leaned toward Summer and raised a finger toward the stage. "Who are they?"

"That's VC's drag family," she replied in a low voice.

"VC had talked about them, but I've never met them."

Summer touched a bejeweled fingernail to her chin. "The one at the right is the matriarch, Chianti Riserva. To the left of her is

Sunset Blush—"

"Sunset Blush?"

"Kind of sweet and peachy. Not the fanciest wine, okay?"

"I'm not judging."

"Next to her is Sparkling Zinfandel, then Hearty Burgundy."

Marquise's aging sound system sprang to life with Dionne Warwick singing "Don't Look Me Over."

"One of VC's songs," Summer said. "Marquise made a playlist."

A waiter in a white shirt and black vest passed plastic tumblers of white wine down their row. Chablis, no doubt. Joanna sipped. Perhaps along the lines of Sunset Blush.

Summer pulled a pink flask from her purse and doctored the wine. "Vodka. My special spritzer. Want some?"

"No, thanks." Joanna squinted and examined the crowd. It was too dark to make out every face. "Where's Caramella?"

Summer swiveled in her seat. "Don't know. I thought she'd be here by now."

Caramella was proving impossible to find. "What's going to happen tonight?"

"Testimonials. VC's family will talk, then anyone who wants to take the stage can say something. You want to move over?"

A queen with a massive sable-tinted wig had sat in front of Joanna. "If you don't mind."

They shifted a seat. The queen turned around. "Sorry, honey. I didn't see you back there. All this black, you know."

The second round of chablis was on its way. Joanna put up a hand to refuse it. The queen in front of her lifted her plastic glass so that Joanna's was poured into her own.

Chianti Riserva took the microphone. She was in sequined black spandex that strained over her ample belly. Her lipstick shone glossy fuchsia. She was the chicest butch grandma Joanna had ever seen. Chianti Riserva extracted a pair of reading glasses from her clutch.

"It is with the deepest sadness that I preside over our celebration of VC's life and our grief over her death," she read. "Today I want to tell you how I witnessed the birth of Vintage Chablis from Bo Milton."

Sunset Blush pressed a tissue to her eyes. Joanna scanned the audience again. Marquise sat near the rear with his hand on Foxy's knee. Still no Caramella. She'd have nothing to report to Crisp. A movement near the wall caught her eye. It was the cook, small and dark against the draperies, nearly featureless compared with the queens.

"I met Bo three years ago. Only three, although I feel like I've known him forever. I'd first noticed him in the audience. He must have come a dozen times before he stopped me after the show. I was on the sidewalk smoking a cigarette. It was hot as blazes out there." Chianti Riserva looked up from her notes. "A warm evening, way warm for June. Now, young men approach me all the time. Usually they want some interesting entertainment—"

A few audience members snickered.

"—or they're infatuated with the drag world. Only one in a hundred has what it takes to be a queen. Maybe fewer. I had a good feeling about this boy, though. It wasn't just his looks—"

Here, again, a rumble started in the audience. The waiter passed another round of glasses of chablis.

"—although they were certainly good enough. It was his serenity. Like he knew this was his destiny. He wasn't anxious or worried. He knew."

"Hallelujah," Hearty Burgundy said.

"And he was indeed expert at cosmetics," Chianti Riserva said. "I didn't know at the time it was from making up corpses. He showed me a few good tricks with lighting. And I, in turn, gave him permission to unleash his inner queen. And I gave him his name, due to his love of vintage clothing." The queen put a hand over her eyes to look into the audience. "There she is. The gal who owns the vintage clothing shop."

A spotlight swung to Joanna. She blinked against it. As quickly as it had shone, it vanished.

"We all loved the Halston," Chianti Riserva said. "VC did, too. It is fitting that it was the last gown she wore."

A weighty pillow of sadness pressed on Joanna from the inside, and the emotion that filled the theater soaked through her pores from the outside, too. So much love, so much grief. At the core of her grief, a blue flame struck and lit. Someone must pay for doing this to VC. It wasn't right. A murderer waylaid VC and shot her just like that. One floor below where Joanna now sat. Why? What had VC done to deserve it? It was so, so wrong.

Joanna whispered an excuse to Summer and slid from her seat. Caramella had to be here somewhere. For a better view, Joanna positioned herself along the wall, near the cook. Only a few unadorned heads peppered the mishmash of flamboyant wigs in the audience. She couldn't make out everyone, but Caramella didn't stand out, either in drag or street clothes. Where was she?

"And her strut," Chianti Riserva said. "Unimpeachable." The drag queen hustled across the stage in a close imitation of VC's stride. The audience cheered, their plastic cups of wine catching the light as they toasted her.

When the clamor died down, Chianti Riserva continued. "What VC had was charisma. Not every pretty queen has it. Maybe they look good, they have the walk, they can dance. But charisma is something that comes from the heart." The drag queen clutched a fist to her chest. "When she was on stage, no one could look away."

Joanna leaned to the cook. "Have you seen Caramella?"

The cook's skin was nearly translucent, as if it rarely took nourishment from the sun. "Why?"

"I thought she'd be here, that's all."

The cook started to say something, but closed his mouth. Without a word, he turned his back and walked toward the basement stairs.

Joanna stared after him. *That certainly went well.* Giving up for the moment on finding Caramella, she returned to her seat next to Summer.

Marquise took the microphone next. "VC was a daughter to me," he started. The next hour was filled with heartfelt odes to VC's gentleness, sly sense of humor, and kindness. Several jugs of chablis were emptied, as well. Joanna had kept her drinking to a minimum, but the crowd around her had gone full-on bacchanalia.

When the last speaker left the stage, Shirley Bassey's "Get the Party Started" came over the speakers, then jumped a notch in volume.

"One of VC's favorites." Summer had to raise her voice to say it. She tossed a wad of tissues to the floor. A smile spread over her glossy lips, and she extended a hand to Joanna. Hand in hand, they mounted the now-crowded stage. The mesmerizing refrain throbbed through the theater.

"I wouldn't be surprised if VC herself showed up," a man's voice said next to her.

Joanna jumped at the words. It was only Lewis.

"They're singing loud enough to raise the dead, anyway. Quite a lot of chablis has been consumed," he added.

"Yes." She was still regaining her breath.

The music roared around them. VC's drag family lip synced the song, and the stage was crowded with drag queens waving their arms and singing. By some genius born through years of performing, they even managed a coordinated dance routine. The song started again.

"Appetizers are set up at the rear."

All at once, Joanna was too full of emotion to think about eating. "VC. I can't believe it," she mouthed. This was their party now. She wanted to be home, with Paul. Her grieving needed to unfurl in its own, quieter way. "I'd better get going."

Nearly two hours had passed at Marquise's. A spring drizzle had kicked up in the street outside, and despite the usual crowds of nightclubbers, the sidewalk felt empty, even bleak, after the emotional chaos inside.

"It's dark." Lewis appeared beside her. "After what happened to VC, you shouldn't be out here alone."

"If you don't mind walking me to my car, I'd appreciate it. I'm parked just down the block," Joanna said.

They walked in silence. Old Town's buildings were mostly iron-fronted and narrow, showing turn-of-the-century construction. The ornate trim had been ripped from some buildings years ago and stucco, now cracking, smoothed their facades. A few, like Imago Mundi, had been restored and were ready for an old western movie's stage set.

A knot of people stood in front of Hobo's, the bar down the block from Marquise's. They didn't look dressed for clubbing in their tennis shoes and coats.

"Waiting for the shanghai tunnels tour," Lewis said.

"You think they're real, the tunnels?" Joanna asked.

"There's nothing in Imago Mundi's basement but mold." They passed an empty storefront, a man covered with an old sleeping bag filling the doorway. A pit bull snuggled against his owner. "Tourist trap, those so-called tunnels are," Lewis said. "That's all. Kind of a shame, though. It's a good story."

They reached Joanna's car, an ancient Corolla she'd named Old Blue. "I'll see you this Sunday."

"Thank you for everything. Thanks especially for coming through for my wedding. It would have been take-out pizza without you."

"I'm happy to do it. In fact, I'll be there personally to make sure it gets done right. Do get back to me with the location."

She opened her mouth for a final goodbye when she heard the voice, a clear tenor.

"Joanna," it said.

A cold shiver vibrated through her gut. She knew that voice, but it was impossible. VC was dead.

"Over here."

Both Joanna and Lewis looked toward the narrow alley between the abandoned building and the design studio next door.

"VC." Lewis staggered back.

"Can't be," Joanna said.

VC stepped into the light for a split second, then retreated. There was no mistaking her sharp cheekbones and full lips. She was dressed all in black, like the mourners at her memorial service. The veil from her close-fitting vintage hat dipped over her eyes.

It couldn't be VC. Couldn't. Yet she knew Joanna's name.

With a yelp, Lewis snapped to life. He pulled away from Joanna and propelled his bulk down the street, running away from the alley. Joanna stared after him only a second before returning her gaze toward VC.

She was gone.

Joanna's limbs finally loosened, and she ran across the street toward the alley, narrowly missing being hit by a taxi. But VC's lithe figure, gracefully moving on four-inch leopard stilettos, had vanished around the corner.

Chapter 10

Joanna looked again down the street. Lewis had disappeared. By the time she made it around the block, VC would be long gone.

Who could it have been? VC's elegant carriage was distinctive. Adele had told her she'd seen VC at their back door after she'd died. Unless — Joanna stood straighter — unless it was family. VC's brother, Barry, was near enough VC in figure to impersonate her. Adele might have, too, for that matter. Marquise said he'd invited the family to the memorial service. They knew when and where it was.

Joanna slid into the driver's seat and started the engine. What would inspire VC's family to play such a macabre prank? No. Joanna didn't believe it. And yet, who else could it be? She'd settle this in a few minutes.

As she raced across town, impatient at stoplights, a thought grew. She had seen only VC's body in Marquise's basement. Not her face. By some miracle, could VC be alive?

At last, Joanna was at the funeral home, guiding Old Blue into a dark spot on the street below the funeral home. For a moment, she had the sensation of standing in a 1950s horror movie, with the moon shining over a haunted mansion, century-old trees obscuring its face.

Drawing a shaky breath, she crept around the edge of the parking area to the back of the funeral home where VC's family might keep its cars. A minivan, weakly lit by a yellow mercury light, was parked by the garage. She laid a palm on its hood. Cold. No one had used this car recently.

Catching her breath, Joanna faced the funeral home's rear. Pale light showed through the basement-level kitchen windows. The rest of the home — the visitation rooms filling the mansion's old bedrooms upstairs — was dark. The adrenaline in her system cooled and retreated. She leaned against the minivan a moment to catch her breath.

There was no way she'd seen VC. Detective Crisp said VC had died. Joanna had seen her body with her own eyes. Her body. Not her face, she reminded herself. A shiver ran over her.

Around the funeral home's corner came a dark blue sedan. Joanna stood as the sedan slid into the spot next to the minivan. VC's brother, Barry, was at the wheel. There was nowhere to hide.

Barry stepped from the car. "What are you doing here?" He was cleanly shaven, but no trace of makeup. He wore jeans and a hoodie. "You're VC's friend, right? The one with the vintage clothing store?"

She risked it. "I saw you."

"What?" His voice was unnaturally loud. The murmur of traffic on the boulevard below sounded far away.

"Tonight. I saw you," Joanna said.

"At the grocery store?"

"You know what I mean." Joanna kept her distance and planted her feet slightly apart.

"Barry, are you all right?"

Both Joanna and Barry turned to the funeral home. Adele stood at the back door. She wore a white robe. A revolver dangled from her hand.

Joanna's pulse leapt in tempo.

"I'm fine, Mom," Barry said. "It's that vintage clothing girl. She wants to know where I've been." Then, to Joanna. "What are you doing here?"

Firearm still at her side, Adele crossed the lot to see them. Her slippers scuffed on the asphalt. She bore no trace of VC's makeup, and given the minivan's cold engine, she hadn't been out. "Joanna. What a surprise." She and Barry faced her, one part polite, one part suspicious. "Sorry about the gun. We've had trouble with trespassers. You can imagine, with a funeral home and all."

Barry looked from woman to woman, then unlocked the sedan's trunk and took out two bags of groceries. The dog trotted from the kitchen to greet him.

"I know this looks odd—" Joanna started.

Adele crossed her hands in front of her chest, but to warm herself, not close herself off, Joanna thought. She continued to clutch the gun. "Barry said you wanted to know where he was." Suspicion won over politeness. "Why?"

"You okay out here?" Barry asked his mother.

"I'm fine. Go on in."

He headed for the house, the poodle at his heels.

"I think I saw VC," Joanna said.

His mother's arms fell to her side. "Bo?" she whispered. "Where?"

"In Old Town. Near Marquise's. I only saw her a moment, but it had to be her. She even said my name."

Adele seemed stunned to silence.

"I know it couldn't have been Bo. So I had to see if someone like him—Barry, for instance—was home." Two bags of groceries wouldn't take long to buy. He could even have put them in the trunk ahead of time. But it would take a while to scrub the makeup from his face. She glanced toward the sedan. From what she could make out in the dim light, the interior was empty. No gown, no leopard print stilettos. If it wasn't Barry—or Bo himself—who could it have been? Caramella hadn't been at the memorial service. Caramella was slender, and her skin, while not as dark as VC's, was olive and would appear darker at night.

Adele drew a deep breath. "It's cold out here. Besides, I want to put this thing down." She glanced at the gun. "Come in and tell me what you saw."

The kitchen was as cheerful as ever. The dog had settled into his basket, and Barry unpacked the groceries. The tiny television on the counter showed a sitcom, its sound on low, and a half-eaten bowl of salad sat next to it, a fork piercing a cherry tomato leaning on its rim.

Joanna told them about the memorial service and seeing VC in the alley. "It must have been a joke. I'm sorry even to bring it up."

"I knew it was a mistake for Bo to get involved with that crowd," Barry said. "He was looking for validation, but that wasn't the way to get it."

"Barry, honey, Bo wasn't like you."

"He was a member of this family, wasn't he? He had responsibilities here. Instead, he spent his nights in that ridiculous—"

"Barry." The word snapped like a steel trap.

"Mom, you have to stop defending him. You and I can't run this place on our own, even with Delilah's help. Bo knew that, but it didn't stop him. It wasn't right."

"We'll talk about this later." Her tone left no room for arguing.

Barry slammed the cabinet door and left the kitchen. Joanna had the feeling this was not the first time they'd had this argument.

"I'm sorry," Adele said. "It's the stress of his brother's death. We're all feeling it." Adele's Nefertiti eyes were devoid of makeup and touched with bruised purple. Even her implacable composure seemed off balance tonight.

"A cruel joke," Joanna repeated. "The service at Marquise's was wonderful. Bo was well loved."

"I know." Adele's voice was quiet. "A few friends have stopped by to pay their condolences." She dragged herself to standing. "I boxed up Bo's dresses. Why don't you take them now?"

"You've had a rough few days. I can come back later."

"No. Take them. It's a step toward helping me move on." She led Joanna down the hall.

With the racks emptied, Bo's dressing room looked bleak. Three boxes, taped and labeled simply "VC," sat stacked near the closet.

"If you're sure," Joanna said. Adele didn't reply. "I'll have to take them to the car one at a time."

Adele didn't seem to be listening. "You saw him? You really saw my boy? I saw him, too. That night. Maybe—"

"I don't know what I saw now. Or who. A joke," Joanna repeated. "That had to be it."

"I know my son. I'll know when I see him." She bit a lip and released it. "The medical examiner will be calling for us to pick him up soon. I'll know."

Chapter 11

"I'm telling you, it was VC," Joanna said the next morning.

"You mean, it looked like VC," Detective Crisp replied.

The crepe paper ringing Crisp's cubicle had sagged, and someone had written "short timer" on his "happy retirement" sign. The Police Bureau bustled with energy this morning. Crisp leaned back in his office chair and sipped from a mug labeled World's Greatest Grandpa.

"It couldn't have been his brother—or mother, for that case. I went straight to the funeral home and checked. Barry had been at the grocery store, and the other car's engine was cold."

"Did anyone else see the victim?"

"Lewis Custard was with me."

Crisp set his mug on the desk and folded his arms in front of his chest.

"He owns Imago Mundi, the restaurant behind Marquise's." Joanna had been expecting something from Lewis acknowledging his cowardice, even if just a message on the shop's answering machine, but she hadn't heard a thing.

Crisp nodded, as if he knew the name. "Could have been a practical joke."

"Or it could be tied to the murder. Lewis collects maps, valuable ones. He said someone tried to break in a few weeks ago. I wonder if the murder could be related?"

Crisp made a note. "I'll check on it. See if he filed a report. It's a tenuous connection."

"Otherwise—I don't know. Every drag queen in town was at the memorial service." She paced two steps and returned—all the room the cubicle allowed.

"Sit down," Crisp said. "You're making me nervous."

Joanna pulled up an office chair. "Caramella wasn't there, though. Lorenzo's her other name. We need to follow up with her." She looked at her hands. "No one seems to know anything about her fight with VC. I quizzed one of the other drag queens and came up dry. I'd hoped she'd be at the memorial service, but she wasn't there."

"We," he said, emphasizing the word, "don't need to do anything. This is police business."

"But you asked me to help," Joanna said. "And I'm getting good information, information you can't get. Like about VC's family."

"And we're getting information you can't get."

"Like what?" Joanna pushed away the paper cup of thin Police Bureau brew Crisp had offered her.

"Lewis Custard, for one."

"What have you got on him?"

Crisp's lips lifted into a smile, then straightened. "We haven't 'got' anything. He called last night to report that someone had painted graffiti on the parking lot side of his building. It said 'killer.' In pink."

Joanna smacked her hands palms down on the desk. "Killer" was one of VC's favorite exclamations. "See?"

"I don't follow."

"I admit it's crazy, the idea that VC could still be alive, but her face was blown away. The body could have been someone else." The memory of the blood-spattered floor sent bile up her throat. Crisp pushed a water bottle toward her, and she took a swallow.

He leaned forward. "Joanna, we're professionals. The victim was Bo Milton."

"You're sure?"

"Absolutely sure."

"How do you know? Did you do a DNA test?"

"Yes." Crisp glanced away for a split second.

"But you don't have the results back, do you? It could have been VC."

"You're right. We don't have the results yet. But that doesn't change my opinion."

Joanna's shoulders relaxed. "Let's take it your way for the moment. If it wasn't VC, then the fake VC — the person I saw last night — must be the murderer. He's trying to confuse us. Spray painting graffiti, too. It's more evidence against Caramella."

"Look, I can't explain about VC. Old Town is a party district. It could have been anyone — someone who read about the murder in the news and had the bad taste to dress up like the victim. But I can tell you who killed Bo Milton, and it wasn't another drag queen."

Joanna sat back. "You know the murderer. Why didn't you say so?"

"It's not one hundred percent sure, but we have a good idea." He pulled a sheaf of papers from off the credenza behind him. "We got back the ballistics report."

"Who is it?"

"Bo was shot at close range with a .38 caliber bullet."

"What did the report say?" When Crisp didn't respond, Joanna pulled her chair closer. "Crisp. Who?"

"Roger Bing. The cook." Crisp returned the report to the credenza. "We found a Smith and Wesson revolver in Marquise's kitchen. It was hiding in a pot at the back of a shelf. Ballistics says it was recently fired."

"Anyone could have used the gun and hidden it there."

"Maybe. We'll see. We have a team on its way to Marquise's right now with a search warrant to look for ammunition."

Roger Bing. That was a new twist. Even so, Joanna wasn't entirely convinced. "We still don't know what the deal was with Caramella and VC. And the ghost. That couldn't have been the cook. He's a lot shorter, for one thing. And I saw him at the memorial service."

"And we may not need to know. Thank you for your help, but it's time to give it up. Leave the investigation to us. Besides, don't you have a store to run?"

Chapter 12

Back at Tallulah's Closet, Apple was helping a customer try on a knit skirt and sweater when Joanna came in.

"These are the real man traps," Apple was saying.

The customer patted her slightly mounded stomach.

"You look terrific," Joanna said. She did, too. Owning a vintage clothing boutique, Joanna had seen in play every insecurity about her body a woman could have, from the common "my derriere is too big" to the obscure "the gap between my toes is too wide." Most of the time, the concern was in the customer's head. Joanna loved the diversity of bodies that passed through the door. Very few of them had anything to do with the pages of fashion magazines, either.

"Own it, honey," Apple said. Apple had owned her own zaftig figure, adorning it with fabulous 1970s caftans and fringed vests. She had a robust following among Tallulah's Closet's customers. "You've seen Botticelli's Venus, right? The goddess of beauty? She doesn't have washboard abs."

"It's true," Joanna said from the door. "Turn sideways." Too many people forgot to examine their profile when they dressed. What looks great straight-on might bulk you up from a side view. Capes were notorious offenders. In this case, Joanna simply wanted the customer to see that her belly was a gentle rise in a satisfyingly curvaceous figure.

She turned and ran a palm over her middle. "I guess it's not too bad. If you're sure—"

A bearded man holding a to-go box came in and did a double take. "Britt. Whoa."

"You don't think—?"

"Hush," Apple told the customer.

The man pulled his wallet from his jeans pocket. "We'll take it."

After the customer re-emerged from the dressing room, Joanna watched Apple fold the knits and wrap them in tissue. Something was going on with her. Her steady diet of green smoothies and whole grains kept her skin clear—usually. Today, streaks of red stained her neck, and her skin had a gray cast. Her voice was cheerful, though.

When the customers left, Apple pointed to the boxes of VC's gowns, still taped shut, stacked behind the counter. "What are those?"

Joanna explained. "I'm not ready to sort through them now. Maybe after the funeral. I'm going to donate the proceeds to an LGBTQ youth group in VC's name." She took the tea cup from Apple's hand and set it on the tiki bar. "Enough about that. What's going on with you?"

"What do you mean?" Apple said.

"I mean, something is wrong. You don't look like yourself. Every time I bring it up, you change the subject. I've had enough. What gives?"

Apple turned away and clicked on the clothing steamer. "I'm fine. Just tired, that's all."

"That's what you said the last time I asked."

Apple turned abruptly toward Joanna. "All right. Here's the deal. I don't want to talk about it."

Joanna's cheeks stung. She and Apple had shared confidences since they were girls growing up together in the country. They'd talked about their first periods, boys they liked, teachers they loathed. Apple had seen Joanna through a few failed relationships and encouraged her to square up for Paul. Joanna, in turn, had had a front seat at Apple and Gavin's deepening relationship and had been maid of honor at their wedding. And now Apple wouldn't talk?

"Is it cancer?" Joanna said.

Apple choked a laugh. "No. My health is fine. I don't want to talk about it, that's all. Not yet." She touched Joanna lightly on the arm. "I'll let you know when I'm ready."

Joanna stood still a moment, uncertain of what to do or say.

"Besides," Apple said. "I'm the one who should be asking you questions. How was the memorial service last night?"

Joanna hesitated. "You're sure? Why don't you tell me now?"

"Trust me on this. Tell me about last night."

Joanna summarized VC's memorial service, ending with seeing VC and the morning's visit to Detective Crisp.

"Astonishing," Apple said. "The whole story. You say the police are at Marquise's now?"

"That's what Crisp told me." Joanna took the dress Apple was about to steam from her arms. "Let me do this."

"It's another candidate for your wedding. A Cahill. What do you think? It needs a bit of repair on the bodice, but it should fit."

"I like it. I'm not sure if it's the one, but I like it."

The dress was an ivory 1960s strapless gown with a Juliet waist and full skirt. Its underskirt was shell pink, and delicate pearl beading criss-crossed the bodice.

"I have a backup." Apple took a 1930s bias-cut blue charmeuse gown from the rack. "It's a nightgown, but it would make a great wedding gown, too." She laid the gown over the bench in the middle of the store. "Plus, more good news. Penny said yes to holding the wedding at her place. She sounds excited about it."

"Oh, good. I'll tell Lewis Custard. One less thing to worry about." Penny's home was modern, but with a rustic Pacific Northwest style including a huge, wood-paneled living room with a stone fireplace. Plus, it was on the Willamette River, giving it a wonderful feeling of openness. "I'll start calling guests with the change of venue. Paul will help."

"I'll help, too."

Joanna picked up the charmeuse gown and held it to her torso. "VC would have loved this," Joanna said. She would have, too. On her slender body, the gown would have held the spotlights like watery moonlight. "Do you believe in ghosts?"

"Really? You need to ask?" Apple's communing with the spirits was a regular occurrence.

"I mean VC's ghost. Could it have been her?"

"Hello, Joanna. I hope I'm not interrupting." A man's voice.

Joanna turned in surprise. She hadn't heard the door. He always seemed to be sneaking up on her. "Lewis." He looked tired, rumpled. His beard stuck out at odd angles, and fingerprints smeared his glasses.

"I had to drop in and apologize."

Joanna introduced Apple. "You didn't have to make the trip across town. I understand. In fact, we were just talking about how shocking the whole thing was."

"I wanted to. It's awful how I simply took off. Leaving you alone with—"

"VC," Joanna said. She turned to Apple. "Lewis walked me back to my car after the memorial service."

"I was terrified. That's the only way I can explain my awful behavior.

Running off like that. Leaving you alone."

"VC—or whoever it was—disappeared right after you left."

"Disappeared?" Lewis half stood.

Joanna motioned for him to sit. "Not vanished, like a ghost, but turned around and ran. I hear there was some graffiti."

"She was seen again, too. By the restaurant." A pale pink satin corset kept bumping him in the elbow, and he didn't even notice. "Someone sprayed 'killer' on the side of the building. In hot pink. I saw it when I got back. The paint was still wet."

"VC used to say that a lot."

"I know," Lewis said.

"You didn't notice anything else besides the graffiti? No one tried to break in?"

"Just 'killer.' Was she warning me about something?"

"Is there something you need warning against?" When Lewis didn't respond, she added, "I stopped in on Detective Crisp this morning, and he's certain that VC is dead." Joanna glanced toward Apple.

Her expression was calm, but uncommunicative. Joanna waited for her to say "He's passed," but she briefly shook her head. Did that mean "no," or was Apple simply not in spirit-communing mode?

"I don't feel safe." Lewis mopped his face with a shirt sleeve. "She was coming after me. I know it."

"Do you want a drink of water?" Apple said. "I can get you something from next door, if you'd like."

Joanna sat next to him on the bench. "If it makes you feel any better, the police seem pretty sure they've found the murderer."

Now Lewis looked her in the eyes. "They did?"

She wasn't sure if she should be saying anything, but Lewis was so distressed. "They think it was Roger Bing."

"The cook," he said.

"Yes."

"The cook did it? I don't understand."

"Maybe," Joanna whispered. "The police are at Marquise's right now."

"We were friendly, Roger Bing and I. Not close, mind you, but we talked sometimes."

"He didn't strike me as very sociable." And if he had been, Joanna thought, Lewis Custard wouldn't have been her first guess for a buddy.

"He was quiet. Liked to read. We talked about books. And maps. Our last conversation was about Tortuga. I don't see him as a killer." Lewis stared, and Joanna followed his line of sight to a mink stole. His softened focus showed that he didn't really see it. "She looked me in the eyes, you know," he said. "Right in the eyes."

So strange that she'd be the one offering comfort. It was Joanna's name VC shouted from the alley, not his. She changed the subject. "Apple, Lewis owns Imago Mundi. He's catering the wedding." Then, to Lewis, "We have a new venue. It's a friend's house, but the kitchen is roomy. Lots of space to set up."

It seemed to work. Lewis's faraway look tightened and landed on the Cahill. "Is this your wedding dress? It's lovely."

"Not that one."

"Have you got something better?" Apple said.

"Maybe as a backup, then. Something will come up. In any case, we now have a place for the wedding and the food. We're in good shape."

When Lewis left at last, Joanna shivered. Some of his anxiety seemed to have seeped into her pores.

She turned to Apple. "Are you getting any hits about VC at all?" Normally, she resisted asking Apple about her "intuitions." Apple might tease her, ask Joanna about her practical outlook and inquire if she had had an awakening. That was how it usually went. This time, Joanna wanted to know too badly to bite her tongue.

"I can't tell you. I can't—I can't feel anything right now." Apple's eyes reddened.

"I'm sorry. I didn't want to upset you."

"My brain is too full." Apple reached for a tissue.

"Maybe it would help to talk about it."

Apple took a shuddering breath. "Maybe."

"Are you afraid you're losing your"—Joanna struggled for the right word—"abilities?"

She rubbed her eyes. "I don't know."

"Tell me. Tell me what's bothering you."

Apple fidgeted with a red patent leather bag, snapping its latch open and closed. "All right," she said finally. "I don't think it's a good idea, but you won't let it go."

The ring of the old-fashioned phone trilled through the store.

"Ignore it," Joanna said.

The phone's ring almost visibly jangled Apple. "No, answer it," she said. "What if it's about the cake? Maybe the pastry chef I called is getting back to us."

"Who cares about the cake? Tell me what's wrong."

"If you don't answer it, I will."

The phone had brought no good news lately. Joanna didn't want to answer the call, but the firm set of Apple's jaw made up her mind. "Hello?"

"Joanna, Crisp here. I need to see you. I want to know more about the specter you saw last night. VC."

Joanna had expected a potential customer asking for directions to the store, or some marketing service trying to sell her ads. Not this. "Here? VC?" She met Apple's gaze as she listened. "Why? You didn't care about what I had to say this morning."

"Roger Bing is dead. We found him at Marquise's with his skull bashed in."

Chapter 13

"Meet me at your house in ten minutes," Crisp told Joanna. "I don't want to talk about this in front of your customers."

Joanna set down the phone. She would meet with Crisp, yes, but not immediately. "I'm listening," she said to Apple.

"What was that call about?" By the look in Apple's eyes, Joanna knew the moment for confidences had passed.

"Detective Crisp."

"What's wrong?" Apple said.

Apple wasn't going to tell her, darn it. Joanna sighed and slipped her purse over her shoulder. "Crisp sent police to question Roger Bing, Marquise's cook. They think it was his gun that killed VC. They found him dead." Joanna shook off her daze and reached for her coat. "I'm meeting Crisp at my place. He wants to know more about last night when I saw VC." Her muscles thrummed, whether from fear or excitement, she didn't know.

"You're enjoying this, aren't you?"

"No," Joanna said with more force than necessary. "Maybe. Is that awful? I don't know what's wrong with me."

Apple studied her face. "You'd better go meet Crisp. You can wrestle with your soul later."

Crisp was already waiting in an unmarked sedan outside her house when she arrived.

Gemma jumped off the couch to sniff at Crisp's feet. With a practiced hand, he scratched her between the ears. Pepper appeared in the doorway, then trotted to the bedroom. He'd be out to investigate eventually.

"You must have a dog," Joanna said.

"Couple of them. I grew up on a ranch, remember." He straightened and looked around the house. Paul's coat, an old Pendleton she'd found at an estate sale, lay draped over an armchair. Crisp and Paul went back to when Paul was in high school and his uncle was a jewel thief under the cover of being a woodworker. "Paul's uncle is up for parole soon."

"You keep in touch?"

"With a few of the old cases, yes."

"Have a seat," Joanna said. She pulled out a chair at the dining room table. When Paul had moved in, so had come a bit of his masculinity. Her chaise longue stayed near the front window — and was a favorite napping spot for Gemma — but Paul's armchair, one he'd made, modeled on a Morris chair, sat near the fireplace. His boots were near the front door, and handmade ceramic dishes complemented her orphaned porcelain finds from thrift shops. But she'd kept the cottage-style dining room chairs with pomegranates carved in their backs.

Crisp sat. "Tell me again about seeing VC."

"First, tell me about the cook."

"This is my investigation, Joanna. I asked you about VC."

"You can't drop a bomb like the cook's death and expect me to be clearheaded."

Crisp paused, as if he were considering how much to say. Finally, he nodded. "All right. I sent two officers to Marquise's. Just after you and I talked."

"That seems early for the cook to be in. Especially after last night."

"Bing lives on the premises. In the basement. But you're right—no one else was there."

"How did you get in?"

Pepper had slinked in from the bedroom and was sniffing at Crisp's boot. Gemma came over to see what Pepper was interested in, then plopped on the floor behind Crisp's chair with a sigh.

"We had a warrant. They broke in"—he looked up in reassurance—"cleanly. They found Bing on the kitchen floor."

"Bashed on the head, you said." Pepper jumped into Joanna's lap. She absently stroked his head. "Could he have slipped and fallen? You said he was in the kitchen. It's greasy in there."

"Possibly. The crime scene team is taking everything into consideration. He'd been working in that kitchen for nearly twenty years."

"A lot of chablis went down last night," Joanna said.

"We'll check his blood alcohol, but it seems unlikely. He was wearing a tee shirt and boxer shorts, like he'd intended to go to bed."

"Then got up to go to the kitchen…." Joanna's voice drifted off. Pepper jumped down from her lap and wandered off.

He shifted in his chair. "There's one more thing. He'd written 'VC' in blood on the floor."

A tingle traveled up Joanna's arms and lodged in her chest. "VC," she whispered. "The cook wrote it?"

"Appears so."

Unbelievable. Her heart was starting to pound. "The ghost."

"Which is why I'm here. I want to know more about last night."

"Water?" Her mouth felt dry. Joanna rose to pour herself a glass.

"No, thank you. You said you saw VC when you were going back to your car."

"Yes. Lewis Custard, the guy who owns Imago Mundi, walked me back. We saw her across the street, next to the vacant dim sum place. She ran down the alley connecting Third and Second Avenues."

"Are you sure it was VC?"

"She had VC's carriage, and she was dressed like VC, down to the leopard pumps." Joanna reached for her water glass again. Her throat was tight.

"Or like someone with access to VC's wardrobe."

"And the ability to make himself up. Like Caramella."

"Let's stick to the story. What did you do next?"

"Well, Lewis took off."

Crisp raised an eyebrow. "We'll need to question him, of course."

"He came by the store today to apologize. But, yes, he hiked it up the street once VC made eye contact with us. Then I went to the funeral home. I told you about it."

He pulled his chair closer. "Tell me again. Why did you go?"

"I figured the person who looked the closest to VC would be her brother, Barry. I wanted to see if he was home."

Crisp nodded. "Or Bo's mother. And?"

"Barry had been at the grocery store. He pulled in just after I showed up. He had two bags of groceries in his trunk, and it didn't look like he'd been made up. VC's mother was home. She came out of the back door with a revolver. A thirty-eight is my guess."

"You recognize a thirty-eight?"

"I was raised in the country, remember," Joanna said, mimicking his earlier comment. "She said they'd had problems with trespassers."

"True. I ran their file before I visited. The firearm is common enough."

"There was another car in the lot besides Barry's. The engine was cold. I told you all this."

Crisp's fingers dropped to Gemma's head as he thought. "A gun. I don't see the mother killing her own son, but the brother…."

"A possibility, true. Don't forget Caramella, though. Lorenzo, that is. He wasn't at the memorial service."

Crisp set his notepad on the table. "We've closed that line of inquiry."

"Why?" Joanna bit her lip, then released it. "I could ask around some more. I barely got started."

"No."

Joanna waited for more of a reply, but nothing came. "Are you sure? I—"

"I'm sure. It wasn't a smart idea to ask you in the first place. And now, with the second death, we don't know what we're dealing with. No, you stay out of it." He tucked the notepad back into his jacket and stood.

"So, what happens now?"

"We'll wait for the crime scene team's report. Maybe, as you say, it was simply an accident."

"If you change your mind about needing my help, let me know."

"It's probably just an accident," Crisp said, but he seemed distracted. "Say hi to Paul."

Joanna watched him get into his Crown Victoria and shut the door behind him. Crisp had been clear she would have no further role in the investigation, that the police would take care of matters from here on out. Despite his talk of accidents, the mystery was only getting thicker. What accident victim writes a dead man's initials on the floor?

Chapter 14

Marquise's call came that afternoon at four.

Not that he called directly. He put Summer Seasons in charge of setting up the meeting. "Marquise would like you to meet with him at the theater," she told Joanna over the phone. "He'll be getting ready for the show. Go down to the dressing rooms."

Surprisingly, Lewis Custard let her in Marquise's. He was wheeling a cart loaded with platters of pre-plated cheese and salami. "Joanna, I'm still mortified about yesterday. I can't believe what a coward I was," he said.

"Honestly, don't worry about it. If my car wasn't right there, I would have high-tailed it, too. What are you doing now?" Joanna nodded toward the rolling cart loaded with food that a man with an Imago Mundi tee shirt took from him.

"You heard about the cook?"

Joanna nodded.

"To make money, Marquise needs to sell drinks. To sell drinks, he needs food. The least I could do is help him out with that part until he gets a replacement."

"You're very generous," Joanna said.

"What brings you here?" he asked. "I'd have thought you'd stay far away."

"Marquise asked me to stop by. I'm not sure why."

Lewis closed the door behind them. "Curious."

"Maybe he wants to hear the story about VC one more time. I never really did get the chance to talk to him. Just to the police."

"I got a call myself, from a Detective Foster Crisp."

"That would be my fault," Joanna said. "With Roger Bing's death, the police wanted to know more about seeing VC. I told them you were with me."

"No harm in that." Lewis led the way down the stairs to the kitchen. "I'm not sure what I can add." He examined the doorway. "They could put a door in here with a good lock. Marquise needs to step up the security."

"At least Crisp will know I wasn't crazy, that you saw her, too."

"Over here?" the man in the Imago Mundi tee shirt said, pointing toward a counter.

"In the walk-in," Lewis said.

Joanna had only passed through the kitchen, never stopped to look around. It was a dim, institutional space smelling of pine-scented cleanser. A row of fryers, now cold, abutted one wall, and open shelving holding dishes over a stainless steel workspace took up another wall. A door to a walk-in refrigerator, where Lewis's employee stacked trays, was behind her.

Crisp had told her this was where they found Roger Bing's body, where he wrote "VC" in his own blood. It seemed like ominous music should be playing in the background, or the legendary "smell of fear" should hang in the air. But there was no sign of anything more than the usual hustle before a show.

"I'd better check in with Marquise," Joanna said.

"Oh, yes. If you'd like, stop by for a drink when you're finished."

"Thank you." Crossing the kitchen floor — squeaky clean now — Joanna entered the main dressing room.

The long row of seats at the mirror was busy with drag queens in varying states of dress, and the air smelled of hairspray and rose-violet face powder.

Joanna ducked by a tulle-skirted evening gown and slid sideways behind the stools to reach Marquise's spot at the counter's end. She could have had her own dressing area, but chose to stay with the rest of the performers.

"Joanna," Marquise said. "Have a seat. I had them set up a folding chair for you."

Down the counter, someone clicked on a radio. Dionne Warwick sang "Alfie." The queens swapped gossip as they expertly prepared their faces. Joanna hung her purse from the chair's edge and settled in under a shelf of wigs. She gingerly moved a gold sandal aside with a foot.

"I'm so sorry about Roger Bing," Joanna said. "It's such a terrible loss, especially after VC's death. I can't imagine how you feel."

"Thank you, darling." With a makeup sponge, Marquise wiped smears of pink-tinted foundation on her forehead, chin, and neck. His cheeks — her cheeks, Joanna reminded herself, now that Marquise prepared to perform — were fleshy. As Marquise patted, her face smoothed into a nude canvas.

"You've been asking a lot of questions about VC," she said.

Joanna shifted in her seat. "Who told you that?"

"Honey, it doesn't matter who told me. The point is, you've been asking questions about VC and if she was in trouble. I want to know why."

"We were friends. I was the one who found her. Isn't it natural I'd want to know?"

"You mounted a mini-investigation, even going so far as to try to hire Caramella to do repairs at your store."

Joanna noted Caramella's empty seat at the dressing table. "How did you hear about that?"

"It doesn't matter. I understand."

"Where is Caramella, by the way?"

"Never mind." Marquise dabbed off-white primer on her eyelids. Now her face was completely uniform. Her pale blue eyes stood in relief. "What I want to know is, who put you up to it?"

A flutter rose, then dissipated in Joanna's stomach. "Oh, I'm through with all that." She had the feeling of sitting below the queen's throne, with Marquise holding court.

With a brush nearly as large as Joanna's hand, Marquise fluffed powder over her face. "That's too bad." She dropped the brush into a can ruffled with others and spun her stool toward Joanna. "I had hoped you'd tell me the police asked you."

"The police?" she managed to say, quite a bit more quietly than Marquise did.

Alexis, a few stools down, lifted an eyebrow. A disco tune Joanna didn't recognize had replaced "Alfie."

"You've heard about Roger, our cook," Marquise said.

Joanna nodded.

"He's been a part of Marquise's for two decades. Not a lot of people noticed him." Marquise turned again to the mirror and pulled forward a few pots of eye makeup in blue and silver. "He was dedicated to Marquise's."

"He was dedicated to you," Alexis said, pulling a nude nylon cap over her slicked-back hair.

"He was very good to me," Marquise said. "He gave me credit for saving him, although all I did was give him an opportunity. He saved himself."

"What do you mean?"

"He used to sleep in doorways in Old Town. I offered him a job, that's all."

"And a place to live," Summer, seated just beyond Alexis, added.

"He had a small room on the other side of the basement."

From the end of the dressing table, where Joanna sat, she looked past the darkened area where she'd found VC and into the rows of Marquise's gowns. Beyond that, it was too dark to see. "He must have been grateful."

"I'm afraid I took him for granted," Marquise said. "He was always here. Reliable. Quiet."

Joanna wasn't sure where Marquise was going with this. She'd called her here to ask something, not to chide her for asking questions about VC. What was it? "The police say Roger killed VC. He was a lot more than quiet and reliable."

"That's it," Marquise said in a measured voice. Beyond her, Alexis had lowered a curly black wig on her head and was fastening a silk rose in its folds. "There's no way Roger killed VC. It's impossible. He was a gentle man."

"Someone killed him, though," Joanna said.

"I know that." For the first time, Marquise's voice was curt. She drew a breath. "I'm sorry. I don't mean to be emotional." She paused, then dipped her fingers into a box of false eyelashes, each lash nearly an inch long. "We don't have a very close relationship with the police department. You, on the other hand"—she shifted her gaze to Joanna—"seem to have something going on. I wondered if perhaps the homicide detective, Crisp, had asked you to collect information for him." She kept her eyes trained on her.

She couldn't look away. Her own father hadn't spent enough time in her life to scold her, and her grandfather had been a pushover. Her grandmother had given her these kind of looks, though, the kind of look that pinned you like a specimen moth to a board.

Joanna broke. "He did." She added quickly, "Nothing big, though. He just wanted to know more about how you work and wondered if there was any scuttlebutt about VC. He had a hard time getting the girls' story. That's all."

Looking satisfied, Marquise shifted her attention to gluing on her eyelashes, one by one. "That's what I thought."

"Twenty minutes to show," someone yelled from the dressing room's edge.

"I have a proposal for you," Marquise said.

KC and the Sunshine Band started in with "I'm Your Boogie Man." Someone clicked off the player. Upstairs, the house would be filling with tourists, first dates, and curious suburbanites to see the show.

"Yes?"

"As I said, Roger didn't kill VC. I know that, despite what the police say."

"Detective Crisp says they have all sorts of evidence —"

"I don't care what he says. Roger didn't do it. He had no reason to, and it wasn't in his nature."

"People's natures can be surprising."

"People have walked through these doors for fifty years now. I've seen more of human nature than you might imagine." She paused to wipe a makeup brush. "I feel that I understand your character a bit, too. I want you to find out where the cracks are in this so-called evidence."

"What do you mean?"

"You have a relationship with the detective. See what he knows. Figure out what he missed. We owe it to Roger to clear his name." Marquise brushed dark streaks under the cheekbones she'd created with pearly peach cream blush. "Given what the police think of Roger, my fear is that they won't give finding his murderer its proper due. They're already talking about how it might have been an accident."

The kitchen floors were slick. Still, the detective didn't shirk his duty. And what about the initials the cook wrote as he died? "They were here collecting evidence, right?"

"Of course. But think about it. They're convinced Roger killed VC. Now Roger ends up dead. Roger is a nobody to them. The police's work is done."

"So, you want me to get information from Detective Crisp?"

"And from here. You might find something here you can use to spur the police to action. I told you I was a student of human nature. You notice things." Marquise turned her face in the mirror to examine the dark line with which she'd ringed her lips. "You have my full support."

Joanna pulled her chair closer and lowered her voice. "I know you don't want to think badly of one of your performers, but we need to consider Caramella as a suspect."

Marquise wiped a smear of lipstick from her teeth. "No, we don't. Caramella would never hurt VC."

"They've been fighting. Plus, the pranks, like the pin in VC's wig."

"Pranks. Exactly." Marquise's eyes met Joanna's in the mirror. "I know both of those girls better than you ever will. No offense, honey, but Caramella is the last person to hurt VC. That subject is closed."

Then why all this evasiveness? Why was it so hard to get to the bottom of Caramella and VC's feud?

Marquise reached to her feet for the half-basketball foam inserts Joanna had seen VC use to fill her dress. "Do you trust me?"

"Yes." She didn't have to think to reply. Marquise was no murderer.

"Then forget about Caramella." She adjusted the inserts and rose. "I've talked with the rest of the girls, and they'll do whatever they can to help."

Down the counter, the performers, now in the later stages of makeup, some clipping on earrings, others enlisting help in zipping up gowns, nodded their heads.

"Yes," Marquise continued, "We'll help. We failed VC. We can't fail Roger. We can't let this fall away." Marquise, her lips rich red now, turned to face Joanna. "You're our best hope."

Crisp would crucify her. Despite that firm knowledge, a seed of excitement took root. Sure, the police would have searched Roger's room, but they were looking for scientific evidence, not the kind of insight Joanna might glean. Plus, Marquise knew Roger's history. Somewhere, there had to be a link to VC's death.

But Crisp. Her smile faded. He'd never forgive her. "Have you tried talking to the police directly?"

"We've always had a good relationship with the police. We don't put up with bad behavior here, and the police respect that. Until lately. Over the past six months or so, they've been hassling us, like they believe something is going on here. They even had the gall to demand ID from a few of the girls."

"After a show a month ago, a policeman grabbed me by the arm and wanted proof I was really Summer Seasons."

"I can't tell you why, but they don't trust us," Marquise said. "They quit bothering us for a while, but it's started up again."

"Detective Crisp mentioned the police were tracking criminals who come to Portland, then disappear."

"See, darling." Marquise pointed with a pink-frosted finger. "That's why we need you. You get insider information."

"You know I could get in trouble for this," Joanna said.

Now completely made up, Marquise stood. "Baby, I can't bury another one of my family."

The dressing table chatter had stopped. All heads turned to watch them.

Marquise took Joanna by the shoulder. "Come here." She led her around the corner and flipped on a standing light. She unzipped a hanging garment bag to reveal a floor-length gown. "Look."

Rhinestones glittered on a midnight blue background. The dress walked the fine line between glamour and kitsch, with glamour winning by a hair. The neckline's daring plunge was matched by a sensible, unadorned hem. All Joanna could think was, *Wow*.

Marquise held up the gown. "What do you think?"

"Is that a Bob Mackie?"

"A custom design. One of VC's favorites, too, although it was too large for her." Marquise pressed the dress to her chest. "A bit too small for me now."

The dress had to be more than forty years and an equal number of pounds in Marquise's past. "It's incredible."

"It's yours if you help. I know you want to," Marquise said.

She did.

Chapter 15

Joanna looked down the line of performers, rising one by one after final assessments in the mirror.

"Roger." Marquise capped her lipstick and tucked it in her cleavage, but her mind was clearly somewhere else. She frowned. Then her features relaxed. She shook her head. "No."

"No, what?"

"Take this." Ignoring her question, Marquise handed Joanna a key. "It's to Roger's room."

The heavy brass key had "do not duplicate" stamped on it. "Is this a master key?"

Marquise rose and adjusted her elaborate rhinestone collier. "Yes. Be careful with it."

"Two minutes to show," came over the intercom.

The rest of the drag queens were upstairs now, greeting guests. Unlike the pageant, this was a regular show, and the queens had performed their songs for months. Other than wardrobe changes, there was little reason to rush or be nervous.

"I have to go up," Marquise said. Unlike the other girls, she wore flat shoes. Still, she moved slowly. "Roger's room is in the back."

Joanna glanced toward the basement's inky depths. "The police searched it, didn't they?"

"Yes. But they're not you."

The overture, a medley of show tunes, started upstairs. The basement was quiet but for the floorboards creaking and the faraway music and clatter of plates in the kitchen.

The lights Marquise had turned on to unveil the Bob Mackie gown allowed Joanna to navigate the basement. She passed where VC was found, the dressing table heaped with cellophane-wrapped flowers and her own branches of star magnolia, now shedding petals. A few roses were stuck in an empty jug of chablis. Long racks of Marquise's gowns, all froth and sparkle, filled the mid-distance.

A room had been sheetrocked into the corner with an old six-panel door and brass doorknob that had lost its luster years ago. This had to be Roger's room. Joanna wondered how long the room had been there. Was it a storage closet during Prohibition? Stories of the Shanghai Tunnels went through her mind.

She tried the doorknob first. Locked, of course. She fitted the key into the new bolt fixed above the handle, and it turned easily. Inside, to the door's left, was a light switch.

Roger's room was small and dark, but more like a cozy nest than a cell. A twin-sized bed backed into one corner with a round side table next to it. Against the opposite wall was a desk with a lamp. Almost all of the rest of the room was filled with bookshelves crammed with books. The books would have been great insulation against the noise upstairs, but judging from the stack near the bed, many with bookmarks partway through, Roger didn't keep them as insulation. He was a reader.

Crisp hadn't mentioned that they found anything in particular in Roger's room. No computer. If Roger had had one, the police took it, along with any sort of diary he might have kept, although he hadn't struck her as the writing type. Of course, she wouldn't have guessed he loved books as he did.

What was she looking for? Did she really think she could find something the police hadn't? Her gaze skimmed the room. Yes. The police looked for objects. She was looking for insight into Roger's character, a crack she could widen to understand why someone would kill him. Or, if Crisp was right, why he'd kill.

For another perspective on the room, she sat on the bed. What did the room say about Roger? The books looked to be mostly travel guides and histories of other countries. Two shelves held nothing but James Michener novels. A globe sat atop one shelf. Funny. Lewis Custard said he'd talked to Roger Bing about travel. Their worlds were so far apart, but they shared that interest. Joanna did a double take when she realized the book Roger had been reading in bed was Henry Adams's history of Chartres and Mont Saint Michel. Pretty obscure for a formerly homeless fry cook. She opened the cover and saw Lewis Custard's nameplate on the flyleaf. The nameplate, engraved, was intricately designed with a replica of the Imago Mundi.

The room didn't have a closet. Joanna pulled open the drawers of a small dresser at the bed's foot. Folded neatly were a few pairs of jeans, some tee shirts, and a few sweatshirts. The biggest part of Roger's life had been in his imagination.

She pulled out the wooden chair at his desk. It likely had once done duty upstairs, had broken, then was repaired and demoted to Roger's use. If she were Roger and wanted to hide something, where would she put it?

Behind the shelves was the obvious place. Joanna pulled out a volume about a Chinese empress. It didn't look like Crisp's crew had bothered to remove the books. They must have felt secure in the evidence they already had. She pulled a few more volumes, then sat on the floor and made stacks of books around her. This was going to take a while. She pulled the last two books from the row and found nothing but the back of the shelf. With the shelf a third empty, it was lighter. She was able to pull it away from the wall to look behind. Nothing.

Shaking out each volume as she replaced it, she looked for any-thing—notes, money, receipts—that would give depth to Roger's life, or to a grudge he might have held against VC. A slip of paper fluttered from one book, but it was part of a Marquise's program, probably used as a bookmark. Another book yielded a candy bar wrapper.

The music upstairs changed to Glen Campbell's "Rhinestone Cowboy," one of Marquise's signature numbers. The performers must have been changing costumes as she worked in Roger's bed-room. Marquise would now be wearing ostrich feathers, rhinestone chaps, and a marabou vest.

She moved on to the next bookshelf—the second of five—and passed another half hour emptying, searching, then refilling it. As she replaced the last volume, she heard a bump, then a squeak like metal on metal. It seemed to come from the other side of the wall, behind the bookshelf next to Roger's bed. Nothing should be behind that wall, except the Imago Mundi basement—and the Shanghai Tunnels, if they truly existed.

Joanna leapt to that side of the room and began emptying the bookshelf. She piled the books far enough away that she could slide the bookshelf from the wall. This shelf was solid wood, not particle board, and heavy. She pulled it a few inches, then rolled up the carpet remnant that covered the basement's cement floor so that the bookshelf would move further.

At last she had a clear view of the basement wall. It looked to be nothing more than a cement basement wall, the corner of Marquise's basement. She placed her hands against the wall. Cold plaster, nothing else. She pushed and knocked but nothing happened, except that her knuckles were scraped by the wall's rough finish.

Sighing, she pushed the bookshelf against the wall. Lewis Custard had a mint's worth of maps in his building. A secret door would be a good way for a thief to get at them. It had been a good idea to check, anyway. Since the rug was pulled back, she continued to roll it back, with the idea that maybe there'd be a hatch in the floor. Of course, the floor was solid cement. No hatch. She'd probably only heard the clank of the restaurant's dishwashing machine.

Stooping to load the books back into the shelf, she noticed an index card jutting from *Innocents on the Ice: A Memoir of Antarctic Exploration*. The card's corner was worn. She pulled it out. The card was covered with tiny notations, each showing a date, then a dash, then a number in small, handwritten lettering. She knelt and shook the book, and gasped as index cards rained from its pages. She scooped them up. There must have been a dozen of them with dates going back seven or eight years. What did they mean?

Joanna laid the cards by date on the bed. Records of money. That's what they were. Roger had recorded dates and dollar amounts, along with a running total. The amounts started out small — five or ten dollars a week. The latest card — Joanna picked up one with a starting date a month ago — showed deposits of a few hundred dollars each. Her eyes widened. The amounts totaled nearly fifty thousand dollars. She took in the shabby bedspread and secondhand desk.

The thought of Lewis Custard's maps came back. He hadn't said any had been stolen, but maybe something small in his archive had disappeared without his knowledge. If Roger Bing had stolen and sold a map, why would the money come in regular amounts? It's not like fences worked on the payment plan system.

Could this be blackmail money? Maybe Roger had stumbled over some scandalous secret and was collecting on it. VC found out, and Roger killed her for it. An interesting idea. VC's mother may have had more of a reason than Joanna realized to search her son's belongings.

If Roger had a savings account, Crisp would know about it by now. Fifty thousand dollars. Joanna shook her head and began stacking the books back into the shelf. Fifty thousand. That would mean a lot to anyone, but it would be unthinkable riches to someone like Roger.

Once the shelf was refilled and the room was back to normal. Joanna stacked the cards again and examined them front and back. Should she take them with her or leave them? Then she saw it. On the first card's corner was a name in tiny writing. She looked at the words for a long time.

Someone rapped on Roger's door, and it opened. Marquise, a man again, stood in the doorway. His face was scrubbed clean, and he wore a terrycloth robe. Joanna knew it was late. By now, the theater would be empty, and the girls would be gathered at Imago Mundi for a post-show cocktail or on the sidewalk smoking cigarettes.

"Find anything?"

"Only that Roger had saved nearly fifty thousand dollars." There were so many secrets in this community, and so much support and love. People walked by Marquise's every day and thought about nothing more than men in drag. A lot more than that happened here. She handed Marquise the index cards.

"Amazing." Marquise flipped through the index cards, noting the amounts. "What on earth was he planning to do with all this money?"

Joanna handed him the first card, the one with Marquise's name on it. "It was for you."

Chapter 16

When Joanna arrived home, Paul was reading a Raymond Chandler novel on the couch, Gemma at his feet and Pepper stretched along the couch's top.

He sat up. "Hey, Jo. There's a plate in the oven for you. I roasted a chicken, and I thought we could have another go at the deadbolt after dinner."

She refused to have a microwave in the house. Their kitchen didn't have the room, and, besides, there were plenty of other good ways to reheat food. So, on a night like tonight, warmth and good smells radiated from the kitchen. "Thanks. When are you going to show me how to hotwire a car?" She dropped to the cushion next to him and stretched her arms above her head.

"Locks first. You have to be able to break into the car before you can drive it off."

"Details." It was so good to be home.

"So…." Paul started. "What happened?"

Joanna told him about Marquise's request that she try to find something to clear Roger Bing, about her search of his room, and finding the savings record. "I'm almost positive he was saving for Marquise, for his retirement. The cook was devoted to him."

It was another reminder that people aren't always what they seem.

She'd walked through Marquise's kitchen a dozen times, and she had never given the cook a second thought.

"Marquise must have been touched."

"He teared up."

She remembered him, just an hour ago, the show over, and his face bare as a scar. He'd taken Roger's chair and sat to look at the index cards. "I can't believe it," he said over and over. *You see*, his expression seemed to say. *He couldn't have killed anyone.*

"Where did he get that kind of money?" Paul asked.

"That's the big question. His living expenses were low — I doubt Marquise charged him rent, and he could eat from the kitchen. But over the past year he'd made some sizable deposits. Not something a fry cook could do."

"Did he have another job on the side, maybe?"

"Could have. He had mornings free. I didn't see anything in his room that indicated it, though."

"So, you're going through with it," Paul said. "Checking the cook out."

Pepper jumped down to her lap. "Crisp has probably already looked at Bing's financial records. The only news would be that the money was for Marquise."

"That still leaves a lot of questions. Just because the cook wanted to give Marquise money doesn't mean he wouldn't kill VC. In fact, he might willingly kill anyone who threatened Marquise or Marquise's world."

"I'd thought of that."

"Plus, the money. I know I said it before, but where was he getting all that money?"

"I know." Joanna sighed and nudged Pepper to the couch. She

went to the kitchen and pulled the warm plate from the oven. Roast chicken, polenta, and Brussels sprouts. Nice.

"What are you going to do next?" Paul had followed her and pulled silverware from a kitchen drawer to set her place.

"I guess I'll tell Crisp. He's not going to like it."

"You found good information."

"Somehow, I don't see him being grateful for the interference. Plus, I'm still worried about Caramella. Marquise is convinced she wouldn't hurt anyone."

"Maybe she was in cahoots with the cook, if the cook really did kill VC."

Caramella and Roger Bing. An unlikely alliance, but possible, especially given the timing of the gunshot. "Crisp is adamant that the cook shot VC, but if there's one thing I've learned, it's not to judge people by their appearance."

Paul smiled. "Are you kidding? You judge people by their appearance all the time."

"No, I don't."

He simply looked at her.

"All right. But you know what I mean." She tried a bite of chicken. The skin was crisp and meat tender. Paul was getting to be a pretty good cook. "You know, they're looking for someone in the kitchen at Marquise's. You could do some digging around for me."

"No, thanks. But I will help you think this through. Let's be systematic."

"All right," she said tentatively. She knew he wasn't a fan of her being involved with the case, but he also knew he couldn't stop her. She kissed him on the cheek, his stubble tickling her skin.

"What have we got for facts?" He folded his arms in front of his chest.

"Roger Bing died in his kitchen. He might have fallen — or been pushed. He wrote 'VC' on the floor."

"Do we know he wrote it?"

"Good point. I'll ask Crisp." A very good point. Anyone might have written the initials to throw suspicion elsewhere. "Bing was killed the night I saw VC, after the memorial service. Now, for tonight."

Paul leaned back in the chair so that it rested on its rear legs. By now, Joanna knew it wasn't going to fall, but it still made her nervous. "Ready."

"Roger Bing was saving money for Marquise, and lately he'd been putting away larger amounts. No one seems to know where the money came from."

"Good. What else?"

"Someone tried to break in to Lewis Custard's apartment. He has historical maps up there, worth a lot of money."

"So, it could be related. Or not."

"When I visited VC's mother, she wanted to search VC's room, but she was vague about what she was looking for."

"What did she tell you?" The chair tipped perilously far back, then forward.

"That she didn't want the police to find anything that might embarrass her son."

"That seems legitimate. If I died, you'd hide my embarrassing things, right?"

"Like your collection of ELO albums? Sure, I'd burn them."

"Hilarious. Next?"

"Well, there's VC's ghost." That. "It couldn't have been Roger Bing. He's too short."

"You said it couldn't have been his brother or mother, either."

She remembered Barry's trunk of groceries and Adele's freshly washed, at-home look. "It's possible, but barely. If it were planned ahead of time, one of them might have been able to pull it off. By a hair." She cut another slice of chicken. "I don't know, though. Neither of them had a reason to kill VC."

"As far as we know."

"His mother was so upset. Paul, you should have seen her. She has an odd way of showing grief, but I'm telling you, it was real."

"What about the brother?"

"I get the idea that he didn't like VC's drag life, but he seems more the type to sternly disapprove than murder for it."

"Don't judge people by their appearances, remember." Paul eased his chair so all four legs met the floor and went to the living room. He returned with a scrap of paper and a letter-sized envelope. He handed Joanna the paper. "You got a call tonight."

Since Joanna had a land line, Paul took messages if she wasn't home. She liked this throwback feeling of community. "Apple?" They had unfinished business. But this phone number wasn't Apple's.

"VC's mother. You'll have another chance to check things out. At VC's visitation, at the funeral home tomorrow. VC's mother thought you might want to drop by."

So, the medical examiner had finally sent VC home. Adele had said she'd recognize her son. This clinched it. The body was VC's. "That's thoughtful of her. I can't imagine preparing the body of your own son."

"Maybe she had someone come in and do it." His fingers played with the envelope. It was addressed to him with a blue pen.

"I hope so." A gunshot to the head. Joanna put down her fork.

VC's ghost wandering Old Town. Roger's death. A queer prickling overcame her, followed by a wash of heaviness. It had to come sometime. She'd been denying her reaction to VC's death for the past three days, replacing the emotion first with her response to Crisp's request for help, then Marquise's.

"What's wrong?" Paul asked. He set the envelope on the table.

"I guess it's all coming home now. VC's death isn't just a puzzle."

He reached over and placed a hand on her arm. "I get it." He swallowed, then said, "You'll be careful, won't you? You promised."

"Yes. I won't do anything to put myself at risk. Really." Gemma nudged her elbow, hoping for a scrap of chicken. "What's in the envelope?"

"Oh." Distracted by Joanna, he seemed to have forgotten it. "It's from my uncle. He might be out of prison in time to come to the wedding."

The next morning, Joanna walked to Tallulah's Closet slowly. Her mind was on Roger Bing. Her discussion with Paul the night before had raised more questions than it had answered.

The morning was crisp and overcast, but Joanna wouldn't be surprised if the cloud cover burnt off to reveal robin's egg-blue skies and temperatures warm enough to coax the sweet peas from the earth.

She rounded the corner and waited for a bus full of commuters to clear Clinton Street before she could cross to Tallulah's Closet. When the bus pulled away, Joanna's jaw dropped. Spray painted in pink across the boutique's front window in knife-jagged letters was KILLER.

Joanna ran to the store, her hand flying to the door knob. Locked. From outside, the darkened boutique looked quiet, undisturbed. Struggling to regain her breath, she stepped back to examine the graffiti once again, and the janitor from Dot's, next door, joined her.

"New publicity campaign?" he said, lighting a cigarette.

"No." VC's ghost had written the same word at Imago Mundi. Here it was again.

Her hand shaking, she unlocked the door. Everything seemed to be in place here — the mannequins posed in flowered silk cocktail dresses, the usual faint scent of lavender. VC's ghost. Joanna dialed Detective Crisp's number.

"Did you touch the door knob?" Crisp asked.

"Of course. I had to get in," Joanna said.

Someone from the Police Bureau photographed the shop's front window from various angles, attracting pedestrians and the occasional barfly stopping by Dot's for a pre-lunch fix.

Crisp sighed. "Whoever did it probably wore gloves, anyway."

From the inside of Tallulah's Closet, the graffiti, fuzzy and backward, cast a shadow on the floor.

One of Crisp's colleagues strolled in the open door, a laptop under his arm. "We got the surveillance tape."

"Put it here." Crisp pointed to the tiki bar. He raised an eyebrow at Joanna, and she cleared a sewing kit from its surface.

The policeman opened the laptop. "Right there," he said, pointing to the screen. Joanna, behind the laptop, couldn't see what they looked at, but Crisp squinted and kept his gaze focused. "It was at the edge of the bar's security camera. I enlarged it and ran a program to compensate for the graininess."

Joanna hadn't known Dot's had installed a security camera, and normally she would have pooh-poohed the effort. Why not just put in a good lock and be done with it? Today, she was grateful.

"Play it again," Crisp said. "Joanna, come here."

The footage was black and white and jolted, as if the camera snapped photos every half second instead of continuously.

"Just a second. Now," Crisp said.

The figure moved choppily across the screen. Joanna held her breath. There she was. VC. Joanna gripped the edge of the tiki bar. VC's long legs scooted sideways in front of the window. The street behind her was dark, quiet, and the bottom of the screen flicked "3:37 a.m." She withdrew a canister from a tote bag. Her arm waved wide as she painted.

"Amazing," Crisp whispered.

"Hold that," Joanna said. "Can you go back a few seconds?"

The technician moved a finger on the laptop's touchpad, and the film started where VC removed the spray paint from her tote bag.

"That's the Alaïa. That's VC's dress — I saw it in her dressing room at home." There was no mistaking the dress's jersey butterfly sleeves.

"You're sure that's VC's?" Crisp asked.

"You don't stumble over pristine 1980s Alaïa dresses every day." For a moment, she was too shocked to act. VC spray-painted her shop's front window. What did it mean? Then Joanna straightened. "Just a minute." She grabbed a pair of scissors and sliced the packing tape sealing the boxes of VC's clothing from the funeral home.

"VC's gowns. I recognize them," Crisp said.

"I'm impressed." Within a few minutes, she was surrounded by vibrant piles of fabric. The last box emptied, she stood. "It's not here. VC's Alaïa."

"When did you get these clothes?"

"The night I saw her, after the memorial service. She was probably wearing the dress that night, come to think of it." Yes. She hadn't seen the sleeves or back, but the dress's body-hugging fit was pure Alaïa.

The technician closed the laptop and waited for instruction from Crisp.

"You can take that back to the office," Crisp told him. Then, to Joanna, "You're sure nothing was disturbed here, inside the store?"

"Everything looks the same as always. As far as I can tell, she didn't come in."

"Roger Bing wasn't so lucky."

Joanna turned to Crisp. "I don't get it. Why the graffiti? Why me?"

They both saw it at the same time. The corner of a white envelope stuck from under the platform at the store's front. Crisp, his cowboy boots sounding as he walked, sheathed his hand in a handkerchief and pulled the envelope from under the platform. It was sealed. Nothing was written on it.

"Is this yours?" Crisp asked.

Speechless, Joanna shook her head. "It must have come through the mail slot, then slid under the platform." The chill of foreboding crept over her.

He held the envelope against the light. "Hand me those scissors." He sliced the envelope open at the narrow end and slid out a folded piece of plain white paper. Using the handkerchief again, he opened it. Joanna crowded next to him. He glanced at Joanna before unfolding the paper.

"Hurry up," Joanna said. Her thumb worried at the back of her engagement ring.

"You did it," the note read in the indifferent type of a computer's printer. "All for a few dresses. You won't get away with it."

Crisp examined both sides of the paper. "That's all."

VC's gowns. This note accused her of killing VC for a few boxes of dresses. *Unbelievable.* She was too mad to speak.

Detective Crisp refolded the note and slipped it into an evidence bag. Joanna knew it wouldn't do any good for her to protest, to insist that she'd never kill someone for vintage dresses, no matter how fabulous they were. She spent the next few painful seconds waiting for his inevitable questions.

At last he met her gaze. "This is about the victim's clothes."

"Her show gowns, yes." She lifted a pair of leopard stilettos from the pile of dresses and set them on a shelf above the tiki bar. She'd tell Apple they were keeping them there to remember VC by. "Bo's mother said I should have the dresses. I'm giving the proceeds to a youth group."

"Show me again."

Still biting her tongue, she stepped aside. The dresses were heaped from Joanna's earlier search for the Alaïa.

He stooped to look at the gowns, but straightened again right away. "I don't see the point of going through these again. You told us the dress VC's imposter has been wearing isn't here." He lifted a Fiorucci dress by its spaghetti strap. "Are these valuable?"

"If you know where to sell them, yes." She waited. Was he going to accuse her, or not?

"How much would I pay for the lot of them?"

"They're too small for you, Crisp, but I appreciate your open mind."

"Ha ha. How much are they worth?"

She knew where he was going with this. She did some quick calculations. "If I sold them from Tallulah's Closet, probably $5,000 in all. I might get more if a dealer in New York showed interest."

He nodded. "Who knows you have them?"

"Bo's mother, of course. Maybe his brother, Barry. Adele might have told anyone who came to pay their respects." She lifted her chin. "For instance, Caramella."

"You just can't leave her alone, can you?"

"I don't think she's—"

"Listen. I know you didn't kill Bo Milton for a few boxes of gowns or anything else. A defense attorney wouldn't be as easygoing about it. Keep your head low. And remember. The last time anyone saw VC, somebody died."

Chapter 18

Joanna watched Detective Crisp's unmarked Crown Victoria pull away from the curb. "Keep your head low," he'd said. *Yeah, right.*

She rubbed her eyes and looked at Tallulah's Closet's front window. This wasn't the first time the shop had suffered a few carousers with spray paint, although it had never been like this. She fetched a razor blade, rag, and some glass cleaner from the back and got to work.

"You cleaning off that graffiti?" It was the janitor from Dot's again, a cigarette dangling from his mouth.

Joanna's patience was wearing thin. "What does it look like?"

"You don't want 'killer' spray painted across your window?" "Ha ha ha" came his Gatling gun of a laugh.

She straightened and forced herself to smile. "Not unless it's true. Got a weapon handy?"

The janitor disappeared into Dot's, and Joanna let out a long breath. Too bad she didn't have work gloves. This scraping took time.

The janitor returned with a spray bottle of blue liquid. "Try this."

Surprised, she took the bottle. He waited while she spritzed part of the "K." The paint melted, and she caught its pink-stained run-off with her rag.

"Amazing. Thank you." She turned to him. "I'm sorry for the attitude. It's been a rough morning. A rough week, actually."

The janitor dropped the cigarette butt to the sidewalk and crushed it under his shoe. "That's all right. I saw the security tape. Any idea who it was? She didn't look like your average punk."

Joanna returned to spraying and swabbing. "No. Could be a number of people."

"Someone skinny, that's for sure. Darker skinned. Not real curvaceous." He pulled a rag from his back pocket. "Give me that cleaner, and I'll help."

"Thank you," Joanna said, but she thought, *Caramella*. Adele had said some of the drag queens were planning to drop by to pay their respects. Caramella — as Lorenzo, of course — might have excused himself to use the restroom, then ducked into VC's dressing room to nab the Alaïa.

Joanna decided. She would find Lorenzo and get answers. She'd ask him where he'd been last night. If she could see him eye to eye, she'd know if he were lying.

The front window cleaned, Joanna thanked the janitor and returned inside the shop. Family businesses like Perez's Helping Hands were often run out of a home. Joanna consulted her version of an internet search engine: the library's reference desk.

A woman with a Southern drawl answered. Excellent. Stephanie knew how to find just about anything.

"It's Joanna. Could you get me the business address of a local firm? The address isn't in the phone book."

The keyboard was already clicking. "Sure. I'll check the Secretary of State's office. Give me the name."

Within five minutes, Joanna had the address for Perez's Helping Hands. As she'd guessed, it was in a residential neighborhood. It was barely nine. If she hurried, she might be able to catch him.

*
**

Old Blue started up with her regular complaints, but within a few blocks the heater was chugging away, and the gear shifts had loosened up. Joanna didn't look forward to the day the Toyota died. They were old friends. She knew how to jiggle the key to persuade the ignition to spark, and she kept a canister of brake fluid behind the front seat. Her mechanic said that the car was "safe, but had a lot of annoying things wrong with it." Joanna had clung to "safe" and ignored the rest.

The Perez home was a modest bungalow that would have fetched a nice price from a Californian couple eager for a river rock fireplace, low porch, and built-in cabinets. But even from the street Joanna could tell that the Perez family had skipped the slavish Arts and Crafts fixings and treated the house not as a museum piece, but as a home. Cheerful curtains covered the living room window, and waves of pastel tulips filled the flower beds up against the foundation. A detached garage sat at the end of the driveway, behind the house. Comfortable but modest. One thing seemed sure: if Lorenzo was the killer, he hadn't done it for profit.

Joanna parked across the street and cut the engine. Her plan was simple: she'd ask for Lorenzo, and when he came out, she'd say, "Tell me. Where were you last night?" She counted on surprise as an ally.

She crossed the street, a wet breeze ruffling her hair. Her shoes sounded on the porch's wooden steps. She rang the doorbell. No one answered. She rang again, and again, no response. A small pickup truck fitted with a rack and "Perez's Helping Hands" painted on the door was in the driveway, but it was possible they were all out on jobs. Maybe she'd come too late.

The door's row of windowpanes were too high for Joanna to peek in. She stood in the flowerbed, careful not to crush a tulip, but the dining room was empty. The newspaper's sports section lay folded near the head of the table, but that was it.

Frustrated, she returned to her car. What next? She still had Lewis Custard and Roger Bing's relationship to explore. Maybe Lewis could shed some light on the cook's activities. He should double -check his map inventory. She wasn't one hundred percent satisfied with VC's brother's attitude, either. But these were thin leads.

A door slamming across the street drew her attention. It seemed to come from the Perez house, but it wasn't the front door. She held tight. Maybe someone came out the side door and was getting ready to leave. Lorenzo?

Barely thinking, Joanna leapt from her car and hurried across the street. No one was getting into the truck, though. She stopped at the foot of the driveway. Did he go to the backyard?

She craned her head around the truck but only saw the garage and a fence that should have been in better repair, given the Perez's business. Maybe the person was getting something from the yard and would be returning to the house. She'd stop them as they made their way back in. The side door was clearly visible.

After a few minutes, it became clear that whoever had left the house wasn't driving away, or walking away, but wasn't planning on going in, either. Joanna crept up the driveway.

A hollow thud stopped her cold. Then another thud, then several. With each thud was a grunt. It sounded like someone was being beaten.

Joanna glanced back at the street. No one was out. A tabby cat had jumped on Old Blue's hood and was licking his paw. She had no choice. She cleared the pickup truck in a few steps, then halted again.

In the row of windows in the garage's door, she saw Lorenzo throwing his whole body into the swaying mass of a punching bag. He wore the same dirty jeans and tee shirt he had at her store, and his hair flopped over one eye. He hit the bag, and his face tightened. Each parry drew a groan of effort.

It looked like he'd been crying.

Joanna backed down the driveway and went away.

Chapter 19

No one met Joanna at the funeral home's front door. She took in the smell of old wood wafting through the entry hall and the armload of gladioli filling the vase under the oil painting. A sign directed guests for the Bo Milton visitation to the McKinley Room on the second floor.

Joanna mounted the heavy staircase to the second floor and stood in the wide hall. A large gilt mirror faced the staircase, flanked by more oil landscapes. Quiet organ music reverberated from the room on the far left.

Joanna clutched her spray of white cymbidium orchids with delicate green throats. They shared VC's glamour. She reminded herself that no one except Detective Crisp knew about VC's ghost's second visit. Or about the accusations that Joanna was a murderer.

She opened what must once have been a bedroom door to a large room with flocked red wallpaper and Victorian-style lamps with glass globes. A marble fireplace was on the room's right, and a small, old organ fit for the Addams family's parlor shared the wall with the door. An elderly man sat at its keyboard playing quietly. One grouping of dark Eastlake furniture was by the fireplace, and two ornate armchairs were huddled at the room's far side. By the casket. Closed, of course.

In the chairs sat Adele and—Joanna's eyes widened—Lorenzo. If Joanna wasn't mistaken, Adele's hand dropped from Lorenzo's when she entered. Joanna hesitated a second before continuing toward them. What was he up to?

"Joanna," Adele said. "I'm pleased you could make it." Even carefully made up, the strain showed in her face. She was used to death. She saw it every day. But this was loss—a profound loss. It showed. She wore the easy-fitting tunic and pants she seemed to favor, but this time they were black silk.

Joanna glanced at Lorenzo and crossed the room toward them. "Of course. I wouldn't miss it."

"Let's sit near the fireplace. There's more room," VC's mother said.

Sensitive to their movements, the organist quieted his music still further. The whole atmosphere was queerly old-fashioned, although a decadent spray of calla lilies in a stand by the casket did whisper disco.

"I know it's a little—it's maybe stuffy for VC, but he always loved this room. Even when he was a child he would take his coloring books up here and play quietly. When there wasn't a visitation, of course."

Looking again, Joanna could see it. No, the room wasn't glamorous, but it had drama. Pure funereal drama. "I get it. Even the music."

"Especially the music," Adele agreed.

"Why is it called the McKinley Room?"

"Back when it was a private home, President McKinley stayed the night here. The decor hasn't been changed since. Oh, we reupholstered the furniture and all, but we kept it the same. People seem to like it."

Caramella was silent. Or Lorenzo, as he was now in a man's clothing. He wore a sharp black suit and blue shirt with a silver silk tie, a sharp contrast to the rumpled jeans and tee shirt he wore a few hours earlier. His hair was slicked back into Ronald Colman elegance.

"We dressed Bo in a suit, but we laid the Halston in the casket with him. I hope you don't mind."

"The police let you take it?" Joanna heard the "we." "We" dressed him. Perhaps that was the final, most caring thing his family could do for him.

"The medical examiner's office sent it with him. We go way back, and the tech was kind enough to let us take the dress. I washed it, pressed it."

This was ridiculous. They were sitting feet from Bo's body talking about laundry. He was dead, and his mother was practically holding hands with his sworn enemy. Joanna swallowed. "That's fine. I'm glad it's with him." The organ's low quaver hummed in her bones.

Lorenzo took Adele's hand, this time openly. The room's emotional temperature rose. He must have noticed Joanna's stare. "He loved that dress," he said. "Thank you for all you did for him."

"Yes, thank you," Adele said.

Lorenzo looked quiet, elegant. Not like a murderer at all. Not like someone to yell at VC in bars, or put pins in her wigs, or threaten her. Not someone to stand in his garage, grunting and hurling himself against a punching bag.

"I haven't seen you at Marquise's lately. Not even for the memorial service," Joanna said.

"I haven't been well." His gaze challenged her to refute him.

"You look well now."

"What are you implying?" He released Adele's hand and passed her a large, white handkerchief from his breast pocket. "Why don't you come out with it? You've been suspicious of me all along."

Joanna knew her words would be harsh, so she softened her tone.

"Why wouldn't I be? Everyone else loved him. You sabotaged him every chance you got."

Adele watched their exchange. Joanna couldn't read the emotion on her face, but it didn't seem to be surprise.

"So you think I killed him out of professional jealousy."

"Your emotions seem to run high."

He bit back a word Joanna couldn't make out, and a muscle ticked on his freshly shaved jaw. "Yes, they do run high. For Bo."

Adele wiped a fat tear from her cheek, but she laughed softly. "He loved him."

"What?" Joanna said.

Lorenzo squeezed Adele's hand. "It's true. I loved Bo. We were a couple, had been for almost a year now."

"But—" Her words quit. Joanna tried again. "The arguments, the jabs at each other."

Lorenzo walked to the casket. The man at the organ glanced over his shoulder and moderated his volume again. "My family couldn't handle my choice of a partner."

"That he was a man," Joanna said.

He turned away from the casket. "No. That he was black and I'm Latino."

Adele glanced toward him. "Sadly, Barry wasn't happy about it, either, but for him it wasn't about race. He never accepted his brother's life as VC. The fact that he was in love with a man? Too much. He knew, though—at least, he does now." She and Lorenzo exchanged glances.

Now Joanna understood. Lorenzo's sullen attitude, skipping out on performances, striking out—it was grief. All grief. "Those are reasons you might downplay or even hide the relationship," Joanna said softly. Sad, but true, she supposed. "But not be openly hostile."

Lorenzo ran his hand along the casket's honeyed wood. "That was Bo's idea. He thought it would be good publicity. He thought people would come out to see the feuding queens."

Did she believe him? If it were Lorenzo alone telling the story, Joanna would doubt it. But Adele knew and believed. Could Lorenzo's anger burn enough for him to kill Roger Bing? Even if it did, there's no way he could have known VC was killed with Bing's gun. Crisp held that information. Crisp, the forensics team, and maybe the medical examiner.

"What about the gunshot? During your talent number?" Joanna asked him.

He winced. "Tragic coincidence. That's all."

"It's an awfully convenient—"

"You think I don't have nightmares about that?" His voice leapt in volume. The thuds of his fists in the punching bag jarred Joanna's memory. He lowered his voice. "I'm sorry. I can't help but wonder if I hadn't added that gunshot, maybe he'd still be alive."

Adele stared at her hands, twisting Lorenzo's handkerchief as tight as the pleats in a Fortuny dress. "The detective came to talk to me and Barry about the cook's death. So awful. When will this end?"

"It might have been an accident," Joanna said, despite her doubts.

"I hope it is. I hope it all ends. My baby suffered enough without having his life dragged out in public. I wish they would close the case and let us move on."

The organist was deep into "Nearer My God to Thee." Joanna leaned over and kissed Adele's cheek, then went to Lorenzo and shook his hand.

The casket was smooth and cool under her hands. What she

couldn't see was Bo's body under the heavy lid, lying next to the Halston's gold silk, so deceptively simple, so masterfully cut. How could VC be gone?

"I'd better be leaving," Joanna said. "I'm so sorry—for everything." It had all changed now. Her theory about Lorenzo was a bust. She was back to where she'd started, which was nowhere.

"Let me walk you to the door," Adele said, but made no move to stand.

"No, please stay where you are. I'll find my way out."

Joanna left the room, the music fading behind the closed door, and let her fingers trail on the banister's satiny surface as she descended the massive staircase.

Barry stood in the entry hall, as if he'd been waiting for her. He gave her no chance to speak. "Still asking questions, aren't you?"

Adrenaline spiked in her chest. "I don't know what you're talking about. I'm here for Bo's visitation."

Barry kept his gaze on hers. "I know what you're doing. We're burying Bo the day after tomorrow, and then it's over. No more questions, you hear? Stay out of our lives."

Joanna's mouth slipped open half an inch before she said the only thing she could think of. "I'm sorry about your loss."

She stepped out. Barry's only response was the heavy oak door closing behind her.

Chapter 20

Joanna finally pulled herself from bed after Paul had left for work. He'd set out a thermos of coffee for her, and she sipped some as she pulled a brush through her tangled hair and shrugged on a full-skirted mid-century dress with a faded purple and yellow floral pattern. Its polished cotton had worn to a buttery softness over the years, and she stroked a sleeve for comfort.

She was so lucky, she reminded herself. After yesterday's full buffet of death and grief, her tiny house with its flowering currant branches in a vase on the mantel and bed still warm and, most of all, Paul, felt all at once immensely valuable.

"Aunt Vanderburgh," she asked the tight-lipped pastel portrait in the living room, "what did I do to deserve such a good life?"

Aunt Vanderburgh wasn't given to a Pollyanna outlook. *Don't forget. You're accused of being a murderer.*

This morning she had an appointment across town to go through an estate before the public sale the upcoming weekend. After years in the business, she'd developed relationships with a handful of estate sale companies in town. Sometimes they called when an estate had a lot of vintage clothing, inviting her to shop before the sale's start. This benefited everyone. Joanna could replenish Tallulah's Closet's stock without the hassle—and sometimes downright irritation—of competing with other buyers. The estate sale companies were able to clear items out right away and make a ten percent premium. Plus, the company didn't have to bother pricing and setting out the clothing.

Joanna never knew what she'd be walking into. Once, in an unassuming Cape Cod, she'd found a clothing wardrobe that rivaled Joan Crawford's boudoir. The owner was a size two, but her clothing was exquisite. The owner's son offered her a crystal glass of golden sherry to sip as, astonished, she sorted throughout filmy negligées and quilted satin housecoats. Sometimes, all she found were worn zip-front housedresses. The housedresses weren't glamorous, but their big pockets and a loose fit were popular with customers. Joanna owned a few, herself.

Today's estate was in Multnomah Village, a suburb with rolling hills dotted with old farm homesteads and infilled with ranch houses. The village's streets rambled and twisted and occasionally devolved into pitted gravel lanes. This house was a Victorian, painted white, with knobby gingerbread molding suspended like tassels from the front porch's ceiling.

Joanna had barely stepped onto the porch when the front door flew open. A harried woman with a phone pressed to her ear said, "Are you the vintage clothing lady? Just a minute, Jen. I said, wait a sec. Come in." Joanna advanced. "No, not you, Jen. I'll call you back."

A baby cried from the house's depths. "Just a minute," the woman said, rushing toward the back of the house.

Two recliners and a television set took up most of the front room. Judging from the large indentation worn into its seat, one of the recliners must have been for a man. It was bare. The husband had died, possibly long before. The other recliner had doilies on the arms and back and magazines crammed in its pocket. The woman's. In the adjoining room was a freshly made up hospital bed. She sighed. The house didn't appear to have been occupied by a fashion maven. If she were lucky, she'd find a wedding dress that had been kept in a cedar chest and a few cocktail dresses that the house's owner hadn't fit in for decades but couldn't bear to give up. Maybe the daughter would try to sell her a wool overcoat from the 1960s with faux fur trim. Chances were, though, the trip would be a bust.

The woman who'd let her in reappeared with a baby on her hip. "You can probably tell that Mom lived down here. After her hip replacement, she didn't go upstairs at all. Neither did we, until we moved her to a home." The baby grabbed at his mother's necklace. "Then we found a few surprises. Come on up. You might as well see it."

The daughter sounded upset somehow. Joanna's curiosity was piqued. She followed her up the narrow staircase.

"Wow," was all Joanna could say. All three bedrooms were loaded with clothes. Racks and racks of clothing. It would have been impossible to get at them all. Not that any of the clothing looked as if it had ever been worn. Price tags still dangled from the sleeves.

And the colors. The clothes all looked to be from the mid-1960s to mid-1970s. Lime green, orange, mustard yellow, and a smattering of tartan obliterated the off-white walls.

"Did your mom own a clothing store?"

"Nope." She sighed and pulled her necklace from the baby's grasp. He responded by slapping his tiny palms on her chest. "Mom was a hoarder. Do you think you can use any of it?"

She'd encountered a few cases of shopping addiction in her years of collecting stock for Tallulah's Closet. Sadly, none of the hoarders chose the glamorous 1950s or charming 1940s but all had fallen into the '60s and '70s. There were only so many double-knit polyester pants suits Joanna could sell.

"I'll be honest with you, it's going to depend. This era had some great princess line coats, and I see something over there trimmed with Ultrasuede that might be good, but I don't get a lot of customers who are into the Brady Bunch look."

The doorbell rang, followed by a sharp knock. "That'll be the estate sale people." The woman started down the stairs. "Look around. I'll give you a good deal, if you find anything you want."

Joanna didn't hold out high hopes, but she had a few customers who liked a bohemian twist in their wardrobes, something a boxy patent leather brown pocketbook or wide-lapel jacket might provide. Plus, she needed time to think. For her, sifting through old clothes was active meditation. While the professional part of her brain took over sorting good wool from the cheap stuff and innovative style from the predictable, another part was released to think. Now that Caramella was no longer a suspect, she needed to reexamine the facts.

She'd look through the clothes methodically, starting with the front bedroom. Whatever she found to take to the shop, she'd stack in the hall. What was it that compelled people to buy more clothing than they needed—or could afford? Hoarding and shopping addiction were considered mental illnesses, but "collecting" was okay. She thought of Lewis Custard's dedication to maps. Where do you draw the line?

She lifted three jewel-neck wool sweaters from the rack, identical but for their color. These were great basics, and they still had their tags attached. Lippman. A good local department store, long gone. She paused at a few pairs of bellbottoms, but decided against them. As she sorted, her mind drifted toward VC and Bing's deaths.

Facts. VC was shot, and Crisp was certain that Roger Bing had been holding the gun. He claimed to have irrefutable evidence. On the other hand, Marquise was convinced that Roger was a kind, dedicated part of Marquise's family, and certainly the fact that he was saving to help fund Marquise's retirement was evidence in his favor. If Roger was pro-Marquise, he never would have killed VC. Furthermore, as far as anyone knew, VC and Roger had no relationship outside of what took place at Marquise's.

However, Bing had been making money from something over the past six months. Bing and Lewis Custard were friendly, and Bing likely knew about his map collection—a collection someone had tried to steal.

VC's only known enemy was Caramella, but according to Adele and Caramella herself, their feud was all show. Joanna believed them.

VC's brother had threatened Joanna, telling her to leave the family alone. You don't threaten someone unless you have something at stake. Barry would never have murdered his own brother, would he? Say he did have a motive. Why would he risk doing it at Marquise's? VC's wasn't the only death. Could Barry also have murdered Roger Bing?

Joanna's hands lit on a floor-length camel knit gown with a gold belt. Not Halston, but elegant. She added it to the pile in the hall.

Then there was VC's ghost. Barry might have dressed as his brother in drag. Easily. Then, knowing somehow—or simply suspecting—Roger's guilt, he killed the cook and tried to cast the blame on Joanna. This theory had possibilities.

Moving to the back bedroom, Joanna smiled. Before her were a dozen pairs of go-go boots in white, black, and red patent leather. All size seven—solid gold on the vintage market. She heaped them in the hall.

When she was finished here, she was going to visit Detective Crisp.

*
**

"You're lucky to have caught me in." Detective Crisp ushered Joanna to his cubicle. "What's going on?"

Joanna took the visitor's chair, while Crisp leaned back in his own chair, crossing one cowboy-booted leg over the other.

"I went to Bo Milton's visitation yesterday, and something disturbing happened. I wanted to tell you. Maybe it will help with the investigation."

A uniformed cop ducked her head over Crisp's cubicle wall. "Party's in five in the break room, Crisp."

"Thanks," Crisp said to the woman. Then, to Joanna, "Go on. You're not going to tell me that other drag queen, Caramella, did something else that made you suspect him — her, I mean — are you?"

"No. I was wrong about that." She gauged Crisp's reaction. His expression didn't change. "It turns out they were lovers. Their arguments were all for show."

"I know."

Joanna's lips parted, then closed. He knew? And didn't tell her?

"You're not going to miss your own party, man, are you?" A thin man holding a coffee mug stood in the doorway. "Joanna Hayworth, is that you?"

Joanna turned to see Detective Sedillo, someone she'd worked with the year before on a jewel heist. He must have lost fifty pounds since then. She rose and shook his hand. "You look great."

"Feel great, too." He pulled an apple from his pocket. "No cake for me at Crisp's shindig. Nice to see you." He continued down the hall.

Joanna returned to her chair. "So, you know about Caramella and VC. How did you figure that out?"

"It's my job. It was easy enough to deduce from the number of texts they traded. But tell me what's 'disturbing' about it."

"Why didn't you let me know?"

"Why should I have? This is a homicide investigation. Thank you for your help, but we've moved on. Now, if you have something to tell me—"

"If you knew Caramella wasn't a suspect, you should have clued me in. I've been running all around town to try to figure it out for you."

"Didn't I tell you you were off the case?"

She glared at him. "When I was leaving Bo's visitation, Barry, Bo's brother, stopped me. He warned me to quit asking questions about VC's death."

Crisp watched her without replying.

"Well?" she said. "Doesn't that sound suspicious? He looks a lot like VC. He could have dressed in drag and killed Roger Bing."

"Why did Barry stop you? Have you been asking questions you shouldn't? This is a homicide investigation, Joanna. Not an episode of 'Murder, She Wrote.'"

"I haven't been doing anything that would get in your way. I simply went to the funeral home to pay my respects. Lorenzo—that's Caramella—was there." She kept her expression innocent, if perturbed. She wasn't finished yet. "I have one more thing. I should have told you when you came by the store, but I was distracted. Did you know that Roger Bing was saving money to give to Marquise?"

Joanna could tell from Crisp's focus that she was telling him something new. "We knew he had savings. Nearly fifty thousand tucked away, deposited at regular intervals. You say it was for Marquise?"

"Yes. He kept a record of his deposits on index cards and made a note that it was for Marquise's retirement. Why would he kill one of Marquise's performers when he cared so much for him? Doesn't that change things?"

"I admit I didn't know the money was for Marquise. But it doesn't matter."

Adrenaline simmered in Joanna's system, a sure sign she was going to do something she'd regret. "How could it not matter? It speaks directly to motive."

"Here's the deal. We're sure who killed whom — positive — so motive doesn't matter. Bing killed VC. Who knows why? Maybe he was worried that VC would make him look bad for some reason. Or maybe he simply got tired of VC bad-mouthing his chicken strips. It doesn't matter."

"Of course it matters." She'd intended the words to come out as part of a reasonable discussion. Instead, they were loud enough to knock Crisp back in his seat. "I was accused of killing VC, remember?"

"What have you been doing, Joanna?"

She counted three calming breaths before she spoke. "Marquise doesn't believe Roger killed VC. He doesn't trust you" — she gave him a pointed look — "and wanted me to look for some evidence that might clear Roger's name."

Anger gathered on Crisp's face, but when he spoke, his voice was low and cool. "Do I have to charge you with interfering in an investigation?"

"Crisp, what's your deal? Why does this case affect you like this?"

"I don't know what you're talking about."

"I called you — not 911, not anyone else — when I found VC, because you know how to keep a level head. But from the beginning you've been ordering people around to the point that you're hurting the investigation."

The detective's expression turned stony. Joanna couldn't tell if he was about to explode with anger or would simply ignore her words.

He examined his fingertips a moment, then lifted his head. "Thank you."

She looked up in surprise. "What?"

"Thank you for pointing that out. I come from a different generation than you. Men who love other men, or who dress like women — well, Flip Wilson was as far as we'd let it go. I guess my discomfort shows. I'm not proud of that."

"Foster Crisp's retirement party is starting in the break room," came a voice over the loudspeakers.

Crisp's phone rang. He glanced at the display, then picked up the receiver. "Crisp here." Pause. "I'll be down in a moment." He hung up and stood. "According to the crime scene team, the greasy floor in the kitchen showed that Roger slipped and fell. He hit his head on the sink's edge. It killed him."

"But he'd been working in that kitchen for years." Joanna was forced to stand, since Crisp was clearly intent on abandoning her in his cubicle. "What if someone pushed him?" Another thought occurred to her. VC's ghost. "Or frightened him?"

He stepped into the main corridor. "Time to pack it in, Joanna." Then he stopped. "The angle VC was found does give me pause." He shook his head. "No. The case is a wrap."

She clenched her purse to relieve some of her frustration. There was nothing left for her to say. "Thanks for your time." She pulled her dress straighter and smoothed the skirt. Then, because she couldn't help it, "Marquise isn't convinced. He doesn't trust you guys."

"Lighten up. I see you're concerned, but you've got to let it go." His expression softened. "We've asked him a few questions, that's all. Maybe he took it the wrong way."

"Marquise thinks you're targeting his business."

"I told you. People—people we're interested in for other reasons—have been seen going into Marquise's, and not during show
hours. We had a few questions, that's all."

"Roger. The cook. He's the only person who would be there—"
Ah. Now it was starting to make sense. Roger had something else
going on the side. "You think the cook was involved?"

"No comment. I'd better get to my retirement party before the cake
is gone." He turned toward her. "And, Joanna, if you see Marquise,
give him my regards. I'll stop by soon myself. I have an apology
to make."

Chapter 21

After leaving the Police Bureau, Joanna wandered downtown to put off visiting Marquise. She didn't have anything to tell him — nothing that would make him happy, that is. Crisp's story hadn't changed. To her, it felt like lazy police work. Short-timer's syndrome must have him by the neck.

Crisp had hinted at the possibility that he was working on something bigger, and he didn't want her to know. Her thoughts wandered to Lewis Custard's maps.

Still pondering, Joanna stopped into a vintage clothing store. Maybe they'd have a wedding dress for her. This store, Xanadu, differed from Tallulah's Closet in that it had a men's section and display cases of vintage accessories, including cigarette cases, tie tacks, perfume bottles, and even a few Murano ash trays. An old pug waddled out from behind the counter to bark once at her before returning to his pillow to continue his nap.

"Hi, Joanna. It's been a while." Ricky, the owner's son, came from the back of the store where he had been straightening a rack of ties. "Anything new?"

She might have said, "Yes, I'm accused of murder," but she settled for, "I'm getting married. Sunday." She lifted a blue art glass ashtray with a satiny depth. Her dresser at home was covered with them, and they were filled with earrings, perfume samples, and bracelets. She'd finally given one over to Paul for the loose change he rummaged from his pockets each night.

"What are you going to wear?"

She looked up at him and said nothing.

"What? You don't have anything?"

"That's why I'm here. I was hoping you could help me." The wedding seemed so far away, but it was happening in only three days.

"You can't be serious. The owner of Tallulah's Closet can't find a wedding dress?"

Joanna sighed. "The cobbler's children, and all that. You know."

Ricky pulled at his mustache and gave her a quick once-over for size. "Come back here. We might have something." After a few steps, he turned. "I hear you were down at Marquise's when that drag queen was murdered."

The vintage clothing shop grapevine was tight. Most of the juiciest information — upcoming estate sales, celebrity clients, the latest rash of *Great Gatsby*-themed school fundraisers for which moms would be flooding the stores — was exchanged at Alcoholics Anonymous meetings, which left Joanna out of the loop. Customers, though, often filled her in. The dedicated vintage clothing customer usually had one or two "home" boutiques, but she popped into the others often enough to gather intelligence to deliver at her next stop. It was how Joanna discovered that her one-time rival, Eve, had moved to Boston, for instance, and it was how she landed the first pick of a local high school's costume department.

"It's true. It was gory. And sad." She looked away, then back.

Ricky nodded once in understanding. "How about the police? Are they getting anywhere?"

"They thought they knew who did it. Then that person died. The fry cook at Marquise's." Roger Bing's death wouldn't have made the splash that VC's did. Despite his rich inner life and devotion to Marquise, he was anonymous.

"Maybe it was a personal dispute," Ricky said.

"No one knows."

"I heard the drag queen's ghost showed up and left warnings, and that she grew up in a funeral home."

She could tell Ricky all about it, but she hesitated. There were too many open questions. "I've heard the same thing. Creepy, huh?"

They reached a rack of long gowns. He pulled out one with an empire waist and a ruffle flounced at the hem. "What do you think of this? Early '70s. Very Haight Ashbury."

"I was just at a hoarder's house, and it was full of the 1970s. I'm not sure I can look at anything from that decade without David Cassidy flashbacks."

"Everything else is the wrong size. What about a day dress?"

"I could do that. Or a suit, even." This was not the time to get picky. Paul had said he didn't care what she wore, but she had her reputation to think of.

"A vintage clothing dealer with no wedding dress." Ricky shook his head. "I still can't believe it. We have two suits that might work. This one's by Adrian."

"I love it." The suit, likely from the early 1950s, had wide shoulders and a pencil skirt, but its chief feature was a keyhole neckline. In gray gabardine, it wasn't right for the wedding, but she had to have it. She could wear the suit to the shop or with a satin blouse for events. "What's the waist?"

"Twenty-eight inches on the skirt with lots of give on the hips.

Twenty percent off for you."

"I'll take it." Adrian, no less. Hollywood film designers had a strong pull for Joanna, and they rarely crossed the local vintage clothing circuit. "Where'd you get it?"

Ricky lifted an eyebrow. "I'll tell if you give on where you got that collection of Gucci handbags."

"Nothing doing." One day an elderly man had shown up at Tallulah's Closet with a garbage bag full of Gucci purses from the 1960s. The real thing. He'd said his brother had died, and they'd discovered a closet full of handbags. Apparently, his collection was a secret hobby. Joanna had sworn she wouldn't divulge her source.

Ricky slipped the suit into a garment bag. "The drag queen who died wore vintage, right?" At Joanna's nod, he added, "I wonder what happened to her gowns?"

"Her mother gave them to me."

"Aha! So, you're the murderer." Ricky chuckled at his own joke.

Joanna couldn't even raise a smile. "I'm selling them for charity." They'd returned to the central display case, and Joanna's hand automatically went to the Murano dish.

"I'll make you a deal on that ash tray, if you want."

Joanna felt the ashtray's cool, heavy weight once again before setting it on the counter. "No, thanks. My dresser can't hold another one."

Ricky waved at a customer who entered, to-go coffee cup in hand. "How about if you set the cup on the counter while you look? That will free up your hands." Plus keep an expensive accident from happening, he didn't need to add. Then, to Joanna, "Forget about Adrian and Gucci. I bet the funeral home holds a secret or two."

Secrets. He was right. If Barry or Adele played a role in either murder, the evidence would be at the funeral home. She laid the

Adrian suit over her arm. The evidence—spray paint, or better yet, the Alaïa. One thing was sure. Whoever VC's ghost was, he had the Alaïa.

The customer was flipping through a rack of blouses by holding the fabric rather than the hanger. With delicate silk and cotton batiste, this was a sure way to shredding. Joanna let Ricky go. "I'll see you soon, I hope."

The seed of an idea had been planted.

Once again, Joanna parked Old Blue down the street from Marquise's, but this time she passed the theater and went to Hobo's, the bar down the block. A dozen or so people milled near the bar waiting for the Shanghai Tunnels tour. She found Marquise and Foxy seated at a two-top in the dining room.

To Joanna, Hobo's felt as calm and comfortable as a grandmother's house. Its brass light fixtures, oak trim, and framed posters drew the older gay set from throughout Portland to enjoy the happy hour steak sandwich. It was the sort of place a young gay man might take his parents without shocking them or breaking the bank, or an older couple might chat with the bartender, an old friend. Everyone knew that Marquise and Foxy regularly ate their pre-show dinners at Hobo's.

Tonight, Marquise was in drag, with a wedding cake of a blonde wig, but no jewelry. Her heavy earrings had to pinch. She was probably saving them for the show.

"Pull up a seat, honey," Marquise said. "Tell me what you've found."

Joanna told her about the meeting with Crisp and his insistence that Roger Bing killed VC, as well as his theory that Bing's death was accidental.

Marquise stared at her a full minute before speaking. "Isn't there something else you want to tell me? About your store?"

How had Marquise found out about that, and how much did she know? "That's right. Last night someone spray-painted 'killer' on my shop's front window. The security camera caught a person dressed like VC."

"Is that all?" Marquise fixed Joanna with her stare.

Honestly, Marquise must be part swami. "No. There was a note."

The old drag queen's expression softened, as if she'd been waiting for her confession. "Yes?"

"It accused me of killing VC." Joanna choked out the words.

"Just a moment," Marquise said.

A nervously smiling couple approached from the group waiting for the tour. "We love your shows," said the woman. She could have been a Botticelli angel with her high forehead and long curly hair. Her drab Pacific Northwest sportswear killed the impression below the neck.

"I mean," her husband added, "it's been probably ten years since we've seen it, but we loved it."

"Wonderful, wonderful. Well, you kids enjoy the tour. Hope to see you at a show soon."

The couple, stealing glances back at Marquise, left.

"You don't believe it, do you? The note?" Joanna asked.

"Of course not, darling."

She relaxed back into her chair. "That's not all. I went to VC's visitation this morning, and VC's brother, Barry, threatened me on the way out. Told me not to come back and to stop asking questions."

"I recall VC saying he had some trouble with his family accepting his drag life," Marquise said.

"Not that that's so unusual," Foxy added.

"A common story," Marquise agreed. "Sometimes I feel like the den mother of the craziest Boy Scout troop in town."

"True," Foxy said. "Although it used to be worse."

"Men would come to me with no other place to go. We could usually find them somewhere to sleep and maybe an odd job or two around the theater."

Joanna imagined the family that had grown around Marquise over the decades. He was known for being generous, and still worked shifts dishing out dinners at homeless shelters.

"Roger Bing was one," she said.

Marquise set down his fork. "Yes, Roger. All that money, saved for us. Dear boy. Foxy and I can't figure out where it came from."

"I saw Lorenzo at VC's visitation. You knew, didn't you, that he and VC were lovers?"

Marquise patted her hand. "I told you not to worry about it."

Joanna waited while a waiter removed the remains of Marquise and Foxy's dinners. "Someone is impersonating VC, and that someone may have had to do with Roger's death. It gets more complicated." She looked from Marquise to Foxy. "I'm not saying it's a fact, but let's consider it. If Roger did kill VC, he had to have a reason."

"All here for the Shanghai Tunnels tour," someone yelled from the other dining room.

"Such as?"

"I'm not sure." She wasn't ready to suggest that the cook might have been stealing Lewis Custard's maps, and she knew Marquise wasn't ready to hear it.

"I don't like it that VC's brother was threatening you," Marquise said. "It makes me suspicious."

"Exactly," Joanna said. "This afternoon, I had an idea. It's crazy, and it's risky."

"Honey, crazy and risky are my middle names. But you'll have to make it quick, because I've got to get next door for the show."

"Are the girls still willing to help?"

A smile spread slowly over Marquise's face. "Let's ask them, shall we?"

Chapter 22

It's a truth universally acknowledged that drag queens aren't morning people. The rental minivan was littered with take-out coffee cups and, given its cargo of extroverts, was unusually quiet.

Marquise had rounded up five of the performers, three of whom were in drag. Mourning-style drag. Alexis wore a black dress and suit jacket, although the dress had a low neckline for a nine a.m. appointment. She said she didn't have any demure necklines, thank you. The outfit was topped by a black hat with a face-obscuring veil. Summer Seasons and Strawberry Crush wore similar outfits, although Joanna had had to drape a black chiffon scarf to muffle the sequined trim on Strawberry's blouse.

The other two performers, Hearty Burgundy and Sunset Blush, stayed in street clothes. Except for their meticulous eyebrows and manicured nails, they could have been accountants on their way to work downtown.

Marquise had stayed home, but he said he'd be by the phone waiting for a report.

Joanna wore capris, a dark tee shirt, and flat shoes. She had Paul's picklocks in her wristlet.

They parked the minivan on the street below the funeral home. Gray drizzle muffled the air and clung to the trunks of the chestnut trees.

"Creepy," Summer said, looking up at the mansion.

"I've only seen this place from the street, but you really can't make out too much beyond the stone fence," Alexis said. She popped a mint in her shiny pink mouth and offered the tin around the van.

"Ready?" Joanna asked.

At the words, the van's occupants straightened and their expressions firmed to alertness. "Ready," Alexis replied.

"You three first."

Summer opened the van, and three men in drag strutted to the funeral home's grand front entrance. They were there for VC's visitation. They'd take care of matters upstairs.

Hearty Burgundy took a final drag from his coffee cup. "Now?"

"Let's wait for the light to go on in the McKinley Room. That's where VC's casket is. See that window up there?" After a few minutes, the McKinley Room lit up, and Summer's form appeared at the front window. "Okay. You're on."

The two men stepped down from the van. Joanna watched them disappear into the funeral home. They were here to work out some elaborate pre-planning for the death of their beloved — and fictional — aunt.

Joanna hurried through the drizzle to the funeral home's family entrance at the rear. This was it, her chance to find the Alaïa and implicate Barry.

With Adele and Barry tied up with the queens, the kitchen should be quiet. She tried the door. Locked, of course. Adele had said they'd had trouble with trespassers looking for a thrill. She unrolled the picklocks from their felt case and went to work on the bolt. As she plied the picklocks, Buffy, the family's poodle, leapt from his bed in the kitchen corner and watched her.

"Don't bark, please," Joanna muttered. She paused, a picklock stuck in the keyhole, to hold one of Gemma's dog biscuits up to the window. The dog's stubby tail wagged in reply. "That's for you if you keep quiet."

Within a minute, the bolt was open. The door handle took less time than that. Joanna was in. She silently thanked Paul for his patient instruction, then knelt to pet Buffy and hand him the biscuit, which he took to his bed. She stood still a moment and listened. Faint organ music drifted down, but it wasn't yesterday's funereal tunes. It was — could it be? — the Village People's "YMCA." Closer, a faint murmur of voices droned. Must be from the meeting room.

In other words, the coast was clear.

Joanna knew where VC's bedroom was, and she'd seen other doors along the basement hall that had to be Adele's and Barry's bedrooms. She opened one door to a clawfoot tub and white-tiled floor with blue trim. The bathroom.

The next door on the left opened to Adele's bedroom. She pulled the door closed behind her. Adele's bedroom was peaceful as a pictorial in a yoga magazine in the muted oranges and browns of Tibet. A simple, unadorned bed lay toward the window, with a nightstand holding a candle and a handmade earthenware vase with a single branch of apple blossom. Joanna lifted the candle to her nose. Sandalwood. The wood floor was bare but for a shearling rug by the bed. It was so different here than the antiques-laden atmosphere upstairs. Very different, too, from VC's glam dressing room down the hall. Maybe she needed it that way.

Scratching from the door made Joanna jump before she realized it had to be Buffy wanting to get in. She moved to the door and whispered, "Hush." The dog stopped pawing.

Joanna reached under the mattress but felt nothing but cool cotton. The nightstand didn't have a drawer. The closet was empty, too, except for the stately but laid-back dresses and tunics Adele wore, with a neat row of shoes beneath. The vague scent of vetiver wafted from them.

There was nothing here that pointed to VC's or Roger's murderer. Next, she'd try Barry's room.

Buffy was waiting for her when she opened the door. The dog leapt at her feet, wagging his tail, watching Joanna's hands to see if she'd produce another dog biscuit. She'd only brought the one.

With Buffy at her heels, Joanna tried the door next to VC's bedroom. A linen closet. She closed the door silently, then tried the next door. Locked.

Buffy gave a low whimper.

"Sorry, pooch, no more biscuits," Joanna whispered. She unwrapped the picklocks again, and was in the bedroom in seconds. Man, she was getting good at this. Again, she closed the door behind her. Curtains cut off the dim daylight, so she clicked on the overhead light. Barry's bedroom — and this had to be it — was at the back of the funeral home. The light wouldn't be seen by anyone coming to visit.

Unlike his mother and brother's carefully staged rooms, Barry's bedroom was simply a place he slept and stored his clothing. It was neat, but impersonal. The bed was tidily made, and a paperback thriller with a bookmark halfway through sat on the nightstand next to a half-full glass of water. Its drawers yielded nothing but tissues and a small flashlight.

Buffy started scratching at the door again. Joanna was tempted to open it, but Barry clearly didn't let the dog in, and he'd be able to tell if Buffy left fur or jumped on the bed. The scratching was quiet enough that no one upstairs would hear. She hoped.

Joanna crouched to look under the bed and made out a dark, hooked form. Her breathing quickened. She reached out and touched one end, then yanked back her hand. A revolver.

Buffy's scratching had becoming whining, then short yaps. Joanna shot to her feet. The yaps were now full-fledged barks. Joanna rushed to the door, but it was too late. She heard a voice from down the hall.

Chapter 23

Getting caught in Barry's bedroom could be a fatal mistake.

After a final bark, Buffy's nails skittered down the hall. Almost without thinking, Joanna slipped from the bedroom to the linen closet next door and shut herself in among the lavender-scented sheets and towels. She had to suck in her breath to squeeze the door closed, and her bloodstream barely had enough oxygen to satisfy her racing heart. She closed her eyes and listened.

"Buffy, I have clients upstairs. What are you doing down there? Do you need to go out?"

The dog whined in reply. Joanna knew the dog could easily sniff her in the linen closet. In a second, he could scratch at the closet's door, and it would open, leaving her face to face with a man with a gun under his bed steps away.

The next few moments felt like hours.

"Come on," Barry said, finally. "I'll let you out back, but hurry it up." His footsteps, accompanied by the clicking of Buffy's nails, sounded down the hall.

Joanna was lightheaded with relief. Barry had to use the back door in the kitchen, which only gave her seconds to make her escape. She wouldn't have the chance to search Bo's bedroom or dressing room—she was getting out of there. When Buffy came back in the house, there was no guarantee he wouldn't blow her cover.

She hurried down the hall as quickly and silently as she could, to the kitchen where Barry's black-clad body stood, back to her, in the doorway to the outside. She held her breath as she passed into the stairwell in the kitchen's corner. *Please don't turn around*, she willed him. She made it.

The stairwell, an old service staircase from when the funeral home was a private residence, led up to the main floor where Barry had been meeting with Summer and Strawberry. Joanna had to continue another floor up. Barry would be coming this way in seconds. She moved quickly, barely breathing, praying the stairs wouldn't squeak.

Heart in her throat, she crouched on the second floor landing and listened. As she'd anticipated, Barry came into the stairway and closed the kitchen door behind him. Hearty Burgundy and Sunset Blush's voices rose from the ground floor meeting room, and, amazingly, even without Barry, they were arguing about their fictional aunt's funeral.

"I'm just saying, she wouldn't want an open casket. You know how vain she is about her looks. She won't want anyone seeing her looking less than her best," Hearty Burgundy — easy to identify from his Jersey accent — yelled.

"They'll make her up. Besides, how are we going to say our good-byes?" Sunset Blush replied.

Barry's steps sounded below her. He closed the first floor door, muffling the conversation. Joanna was dizzy with relief.

Other than let Marquise's girls practice their acting ability and satisfy Joanna's nosiness, this idea had been a bust. No Alaïa, no nothing. Except the revolver. But Crisp was sure that it was Roger's gun that killed VC, and they surely held that one as evidence. Carefully, she rose to standing.

She checked her watch. In another ten minutes, the crew would reassemble in the parking lot to leave. She was on the second floor. If she passed through to the hall, past the mansion's old bedrooms that were now visitation rooms, including the McKinley Room, she might slip down the main staircase and out the front door without being seen.

She opened the door, expecting to be in the hall, but she was in a dark laboratory-like setting with a running fan and a strong smell of formaldehyde. Her eyes widened. The embalming room, had to be. Shoot.

The blinds were drawn, and through slivers of light she made out the room's features. A long porcelain-enameled table lay near the wall to her left. Thankfully, it lay empty, and the counters lining the wall behind it were tidy, too, with only a stainless steel tray with a box of latex gloves and a few tools that looked curiously like picklocks. On her right was a gurney and another row of shelves. She tiptoed closer. "Dancing Queen," barely muffled by the fan, drifted in from the McKinley room's organ next door. Undoubtedly, Summer was at the keyboard. On the shelves were a curling iron and a couple of bottles of hairspray. This had to be where they made up the bodies.

Repelled, Joanna backed up, knocking over a freestanding metal table. She gasped as large glass bottles labeled Lyf-Lyk crashed to the floor, spilling carmine red, rich pink, and flesh-toned liquids across the tile floor. The Mardi Gras waves of color were violent, but nothing compared to the noise that echoed through the tile and stainless steel room. Joanna froze. How would she get out of this one?

The organ music halted, and, at the same time, steps ran up the back stairs. Joanna looked from doorway to doorway, unsure of which way to run—back to the service staircase, or through the embalming room to the hall?

The visitation rooms. That was the best direction. She'd rather face Adele than Barry, and the girls visiting VC in the McKinley Room would help. Trembling, she leapt toward the hall door and felt a foot give way on the cosmetics-slickened floor. She flailed for something to steady her and grabbed the edge of some kind of machinery on a rolling tray just as both doors to the embalming room opened. She crashed to the ground, taking the machinery with her. Pain stabbed her right knee.

Barry stood between her and the backstairs entrance, his face lit with rage. Adele, now backed by three drag queens, stood at the hall entrance. Adele clicked a bank of light switches, and the antiseptic glare of fluorescent light flooded the room.

Alexis pulled a cellphone from her purse. Their backup plan. She was calling Crisp. Any way this ended would not be good.

"You! What are you doing here?" Barry yelled.

She would not make excuses. This was the plan. Their Hail Mary.

Joanna pulled herself to sitting and wiped a viscous smear of red from her shirt. Her knee throbbed from the fall. "I know what you did." She kept most of the tremor from her voice.

The seconds she'd spent in the linen closet downstairs were nothing compared to this. Her breathing — and even heartbeat, she'd swear it — froze as she waited for a response.

Barry clenched his fists at his side. The gun was downstairs, Joanna reminded herself as she struggled to breathe. She had witnesses to anything he might do or say.

Adele calmly opened a cupboard and withdrew a box of wipes. She handed it to Joanna. "It had to happen," she said.

Barry's gaze darted like that of a cornered animal. "Okay, I did it," he said so quickly that his words were barely intelligible.

Summer held up her cellphone. It was recording, Joanna knew.

"Did what?" Joanna pressed.

"You know," Barry said.

"Honey, don't talk. You don't have to say anything."

"Mom, let me handle this." He drew a deep breath. "I dressed as VC and went to Marquise's."

"And what?" With Hearty Burgundy's help, Joanna pulled herself to standing. Lord, that knee ached.

Another pause.

"And what?" Summer repeated. The boys had come up the rear staircase, behind Barry.

"And killed the cook," Barry said. He glanced at his mother. "I dressed as VC and went and killed the cook."

"No, you didn't," Adele said calmly. "It was an accident, that's all."

Joanna leaned against the wall for support. Barry, feet planted apart, was trapped between Hearty Burgundy and Sunset Blush on the service staircase behind him. Alexis, Summer, and Strawberry Crush blockaded the door to the hall and visitation rooms. They'd done it. They'd found VC's ghost and Roger's killer.

Just then, the image of VC's ghost running down the alley in leopard stilettos flashed through Joanna's brain. The ghost had the grace of a runway model. Now she understood. Adele was right. Barry didn't do it. There was no way Barry could run in those heels.

"You'll have the chance to tell the police more about that, Adele. After they arrest you."

Chapter 24

They gathered in the funeral home's chapel, a long room that had once been the mansion's living and dining rooms. A marble fireplace dominated one end of the rectangular space, and a low stage with a lectern and pedestal for a casket filled the other side. A long row of windows covered in filmy curtains ran up the room's side.

Joanna, Adele, Barry, and five drag queens — three in drag, and two in street clothes — sat in the chapel's chairs. Detective Crisp stood. Another policeman took notes. This time, there was no vodka bottle to pass down the aisle. The drag queens looked like coffee might be what they'd prefer, anyway, and Summer had mentioned something about going out for chicken and waffles.

As soon as Crisp had arrived, Joanna gave him a "don't mess this up, too" stare. He'd visibly softened.

"Listen to me," Adele said.

"Mom —" Barry started.

"No, Barry. I'm going to tell the truth. We're not letting the tragedies snowball."

"Ms. Milton," Crisp said. "Please go ahead."

"Mom, at least wait until we get a lawyer."

"Your son's right. You don't have to talk now. We'll need to take you to the station, but you can wait there for your attorney."

"No. I want to talk. The truth needs to come out."

The queens looked at each other. Joanna thought Summer might be taking measure of Adele's tunic for possible reproduction. Joanna flexed her knee and winced.

"Fine. Tell me about Roger Bing."

Adele could have been royalty in another life. She was calm. Proud. She had something awful to do, and she would do it, because it was right.

"When my son died, I was distraught."

"Naturally, you were upset. Any mother—" Barry started.

Joanna had to give him credit for trying, but Adele cut him off.

"Right. You're saying the right words, but you don't understand. Can't. The day after his death, after the police searched his room, I looked at Bo's gowns and thought about what a wonderful son he'd been."

Joanna glanced at Barry. He was listening, but she couldn't read emotion in his expression. Maybe it was a funeral director thing. You learn to shift to neutral when emotion gets ugly.

The policeman scribbled notes while Adele talked. "I tried on one of his dresses, then another. I felt closer to my son that way. It might sound funny to you, but dressed in his clothes, I made him come alive just a little."

The drag queens listened intently. Except for the scratching of a pen, the room was silent.

"I called the medical examiner's office. We've worked with them for years, of course. I wanted to know about Bo. How he was killed. What they found." She looked at Joanna. "Joanna told me a little, but the ME's office would know for sure."

"They told you?" Crisp said. Joanna couldn't blame him for looking irritated, but he needed to stay cool.

"They told me he was shot with a gun registered to the cook at Marquise's. The night of his memorial service, I—" Adele leaned forward, her face in her hands. Her whole body shook as if she were sobbing, but she was quiet. Barry moved next to her and put his arm around her.

"I dressed as VC that night. Honestly, I felt possessed. All the rage and sadness...."

"Grief is tricky emotion," the note-taking policeman offered. Crisp shot him a warning look. He returned to his notebook.

"Yes. I had to see where my son was killed. I spray painted the side of the building—I hardly remember what I wrote—then went to Marquise's. Bo's memorial service was still going on. The music was loud. No one saw me when I went downstairs."

She stopped. They all waited for her to resume. She'd said so much already. She'd surely continue.

"He was there. The cook. The man who killed my son. I didn't expect to see him."

This was the important moment. Would she say what happened? Or would she wait?

"I was so angry. My vision was full of blood. I couldn't see. At all. I remember grabbing the counter behind me." Another moment passed. Her voice dropped. "When my vision cleared, he was on the ground. Bleeding. It was like someone had doused me with ice water. I realized where I was and what had happened...."

Crisp said gently, "You pushed him?"

"No. No, he fell. He saw me and fell. He must have."

The scent of lilies seemed to emerge from nowhere, and for a moment the fragrance was almost stifling. Maybe the scent had been there all along, but Joanna had been too distracted to notice. She never wanted to smell lilies again.

"Then I ran away. I saw Joanna and another man across the street. Right after that."

No one must have gone downstairs after the memorial service. Bing's body had lain on the kitchen floor all night and into the next morning. But Adele had been in a bathrobe with no makeup when Joanna had seen her back at the funeral home. "How did you change so fast?"

"As a model, I could change my clothes and clean my face in seconds."

"The Alaïa. You wore it when you came to Tallulah's Closet, too." Joanna studied Adele's face. The mask was off, and pure emotion played on her features. Joanna saw grief and pain and desperation. Joanna shifted her gaze to Crisp, who nodded once to let her know she could go ahead with her questions.

"How did you get downtown? Barry had the sedan, and the minivan hadn't been driven," Joanna said.

"VC's Mustang. I drove that. He kept it in the garage with the hearse."

"I see."

"I'm sorry," Adele whispered. "After the cook died, I—I didn't know what to do. I spray painted your store and blamed you for his death. That was wrong."

"I thought it was Barry at first," Joanna said. Strangely, she wasn't angry at Adele. She felt only pity.

"I know, honey," Adele said. "He's had enough to contend with. My responsible boy." She turned to hug him. After a moment, she swallowed and pulled back. "So. You'll take me away?"

*
**

The next morning, Joanna arrived just as Apple was setting out the sandwich board for Tallulah's Closet.

"Oh, good," Apple said. "I was going to call you." Smudges darkened the skin under her eyes, and her lace-trimmed muslin dress wrinkled toward the hem. Apple's style was bohemian, but she was usually particular about keeping sharp.

Joanna followed her into the shop. "I figured I'd better finally choose a dress. Is the Cahill still here? If I play down my hair, it might work." She wasn't sure how to approach Apple again about whatever bothered her. Apple had been adamant she wasn't going to talk about it.

"Never fear." Apple pointed to a mannequin toward the store's rear. "That, my friend, is your wedding dress. It came in last night just before closing. " A floor-length ecru lace gown from the 1930s with a modest train clung to the mannequin's curves. Dozens of lace-covered buttons ran up its front to a Peter Pan collar. Its long sleeves ended in points at the wrists.

Apple was right. Joanna loved it. "It's amazing. Absolutely perfect."

"Try it on," Apple said. She was already slipping it from the mannequin.

Joanna held the dress to her body and looked in the large gilt mirror at the store's rear. The gown was elegant, but not precious, sinuous yet simple, glamorous but not too much for a late morning wedding. "Do you think it will fit? I doubt the lace gives, even on the bias."

"I look at you every day. This dress will fit perfectly. As soon as I saw it, I knew it was the one for you." She touched a sleeve. "A really sweet guy brought it in. A bus driver, still in his uniform. He said the dress belonged to his grandmother."

Joanna lay the gown over the zebra-print armchair. She couldn't wait any longer. "I love the dress. It's exactly what I wanted. But you have to tell me what's wrong. I can't stand seeing you like this."

Apple walked to the front of the store and looked down the street, as if she were willing customers to come in. She turned to face Joanna. "I don't want to talk about it."

"Tell me."

Apple clenched her hands. "No. I really don't want to go there. Not with your wedding tomorrow. Plus Bo's death. You have enough to deal with."

Joanna pulled Apple by the arm to the store's central bench. "Sit down," she commanded. "You told me you're not dying."

Apple choked off a laugh. "My health is fine."

"Then what?"

Apple sat mute.

"Listen, we've been friends practically our whole lives." Apple turned away, and Joanna pulled her shoulders to face her. "You've helped me through my toughest times, from when Grandma died to all the drama with Paul, to being poisoned when it was meant for me. You even found my wedding dress." She looked at the flowing lace. "I can't ignore the fact that something is bothering you. You have to tell me."

"But your wedding—"

"Nothing's going to ruin the wedding. It's a simple event, and it's all planned out. I'll be happy, no matter what. Now, talk."

"I'm going to cry."

Joanna reached behind the tiki counter and pulled out a box of tissues. "Ready?"

Apple clutched the box and looked toward her lap. Her lips parted, but she said nothing.

"Spill it, Apple. Tell me." Joanna kept her voice soft but insistent. "Whatever it is, we can deal with it together."

Apple rested her head in her hands, covering her eyes. "Gavin left me."

"What?" Joanna dropped to the bench next to her. "Are you sure?"

"You think I'm not sure?" She pressed a tissue to each eye. "Last week. He said it 'wasn't working' and moved to a yurt."

This was incredible. They'd always been such a solid couple. Gavin was devoted to Apple. Joanna searched the boutique as if answers could be found among the d'Orsay pumps and pastel scarves. In her shock, all she could say was, "A yurt?"

Apple began to sob quietly.

"Tell me about it." She bit her lip. "If you want to."

"Things haven't been right for a year now, but I thought we could work it out. Gavin hates his job, and I've tried to be encouraging, but it didn't help. He just moped around the house. Then one day I discovered he hadn't been into work for two weeks."

"He hadn't told you?"

"Hadn't said a thing. I found out by accident. I had left work early—you remember a couple of weeks ago when you said you'd close up?"

Joanna nodded.

"I stopped by the art supply store. When I came out, he was leaving the bar next door. I asked him what he was doing, and we got into a big fight. Right there on the street." She almost laughed, but it flashed to tears. When she quieted, she said, "I threw a pot of gesso at him. He'll never get that shirt clean."

Two weeks? And Apple hadn't told her any of this because of the wedding. "He's just depressed over his job. So he's touchy. It's a guy thing. He wants to provide—you know, the caveman thing—but he hated his work. So he's distancing himself, because he feels like a failure. He'll be back. You'll see."

Apple watched her with what initially looked like hope but disintegrated again into grief. "I wish it were just that. I think—he might—" Unable to finish the words, she looked to her lap.

Uh-oh. "Someone else?"

The bell at the front door rang, and almost simultaneously Apple slipped to the store's bathroom beyond the jewelry counter.

A couple came in, holding hands. The woman, a tiny brunette with spiky dark hair, waved with her free hand.

"Is there anything special you're looking for?" Joanna asked, rising from the bench.

"A wedding dress. We're getting married." The woman beamed at her fiancé. She dropped his hand and in a few steps was at the lace gown Apple had found for Joanna. "I love this. What about this?"

"It's for me, actually," Joanna said. "My wedding." For once, the words were bittersweet. She realized how much her and Apple's lives intertwined, like sisters. She couldn't be completely happy when Apple was so unhappy, and Apple knew this. It's why she'd kept her secret for so long. "It would be too big for you, anyway. Let me show you a few other options. We have a really nice Cahill."

Chapter 25

Joanna sleepwalked through the next morning. In the tradition of the groom not seeing the bride on their wedding day until the ceremony, Paul had spent the night with family. She and Apple had stayed up late watching *Auntie Mame* and *Father of the Bride*, and Joanna had even convinced Apple to try a martini. It was a throwback to earlier years when Joanna would join slumber parties at Apple's house. Sometimes they had pitched a tent in the backyard to get away from Apple's many brothers, and they'd talk until they fell asleep snug in their sleeping bags.

Last night they'd also talked, but instead of chasing dreams about their lives to come, talk had eventually drifted to marriage.

"How do you feel about the wedding?" Apple had asked. "Any last minute jitters?"

Joanna considered this. "No. I mean, the logistics have been more difficult than I'd planned, but as far as the wedding itself goes—it feels surprisingly easy. Inevitable, even. Like it has always been going to happen, but it took me until last winter to recognize what was so obvious. Do you know what I mean?"

The television was off, and the finished basement—nicknamed the "TV pit" by Paul—was dark except for a candle and the pendant lamp in the corner. Joanna couldn't quite make out Apple's expression.

"I've felt that," Apple said.

"I'm sorry," Joanna whispered. "I hope Gavin works his problems out before he wrecks the best thing that ever happened to him."

"Let's not talk about that. Tell me about the ceremony. Did you write your vows?"

"I did."

The ceremony's highlight was that the Mother Superior of a convent Joanna had helped out the year before was going to officiate. Her brand of the church was flexible about vows, and she encouraged Joanna to come up with something that didn't include the word "obey."

"Did you memorize them?" Apple asked.

"They weren't that hard to memorize." She'd spent hours drafting one set of vows after another, tossing each draft because it felt too stiff or too precious. Finally, she wrote down what was at her heart's core. "They're simple. 'I vow to be who I truly am, and I will love you for who you truly are.' Do you think that's enough?"

Pepper, who'd been lounging on the couch between them, jumped down and went up the stairs, probably to bed.

"I'm not sure what I'd add," Apple said. "Being loved is knowing you're valued for exactly who you are, not who you are despite something."

"Exactly." It was a miracle to love and be loved like that. It had taken her too long to trust it. She was so lucky. "Despite being cranky in the morning, for instance."

"Or despite not wanting to go camping."

"Or be campy," Joanna had said, thinking of the girls at Marquise's. Memories of VC drifted back into her mind. Tomorrow would be a week since she'd found VC's body.

Not long after their conversation, Joanna had left Apple to the guest room and had gone to her own bed for a restless night.

Now it was breakfast. Joanna would don her wedding gown, and they'd drive to Penny's house on the river for the ceremony.

"You're distracted." Apple set down a half-eaten muffin.

"I just can't shake the feeling that I'm missing something."

"For the wedding? I know it was rough over the past week with the food and venue, but we're set now. I even got you a great cake."

"No, the deaths." Joanna finished her cup of coffee. Apple had produced a quiche, fruit salad, and a plate of bacon, but a few bites of toast were all she could manage. "Why did VC die? It's never been explained."

"And it may never be. Save your speculation for another day. This morning you're getting married."

"You're distracted, too. You've barely eaten."

"I'm not very hungry." Apple's smile looked forced. "Must be excitement about the ceremony."

The thread that held sympathy for Apple's pain tightened. "I'm sorry." Then, another thought. "Gavin won't be there, will he?"

"It's nothing to worry you, but, no, we talked about it. He's staying home."

"In the yurt." Joanna shook her head. "Serves him right."

"The yurt's not so bad," Apple said. She rose and cleared their plates. "At least it's a beautiful morning."

And it was. Portland's springs were unpredictable. Here, old sayings about April showers and May flowers might as well incorporate stanzas about last minute blizzards and blistering sunburns. Today, though, was classic spring. The Mother Goose colors of tulips and daffodils nodded in front yards, and a storybook blue sky spread over it all. At Penny's house, people would be setting up the chairs for the ceremony, and the caterers would be unloading in the kitchen.

And VC was dead, but no one knew why. That wasn't right.

Apple, hands on hips, looked at her. "You need to get dressed."

"I suppose so." She didn't move.

Apple sighed. "Come on. You can tell me about it while you get dressed."

Joanna gave Apple an apologetic hug before following her to the bedroom, where her wedding dress hung from the door. A full-length ivory slip lay over the coverlet, with Pepper curled up on its bodice. "Come on, kitty. You can sleep on the quilt."

The cat stretched his front legs and took his time settling by the pillows.

"So, what's bothering you? Everything's pretty well wrapped up," Apple said. "Keep on your kimono. We'll do your hair and makeup first."

Joanna sat at the dressing table, and clicked on the poodle-shaped lamp she'd fitted with one of the warm-light bulbs VC had brought to the shop. "It doesn't feel right."

Apple took up a brush. "Just because you're unsettled doesn't mean the murders aren't. Justice is done."

"I know. But why did Roger Bing kill VC? That's what bothers me most." Her head pulled back with each stroke of the brush.

"Good grief." Apple's eyes met hers in the dressing table's mirror. "You won't quit until you have it all laid out. Then let's walk it through. Start with VC. Do you really know what happened to VC?"

Joanna shivered. "She was shot. Killed."

Apple pulled Joanna's hair up and fastened it with an elastic band before reaching for the Murano glass bowl of bobby pins. "Was there anything odd about it? Anything the police can't explain?"

"Yes. I don't know what to make of it, though." Something fluttered inside her. She was getting closer to the heart of the problem. "Crisp said that according to the medical examiner, VC would have been facing away from the center of the room when she was shot. The only way that could have happened is if Roger waited for her, hidden near the wall."

"What do you know about Roger?" Apple had fashioned Joanna's hair into an almost pre-Raphaelite up-do with loose curls.

"He was a competent fry cook. He liked to read travel stories. He felt a huge debt of gratitude to Marquise, to the point where he was saving money to make Marquise's retirement more comfortable. Lately, he'd been getting money from somewhere else, too."

"A second job?" Her work with Joanna's hair done, Apple sat on the bed and absently petted Pepper. "Your makeup. You need to do your makeup, Jo."

Joanna turned back to the mirror and uncapped a bottle of toner to swab her face. "Crisp told me they'd been watching Marquise's. They'd tracked some criminal kingpin to Old Town, then he disappeared. They gave up after a few days."

"So maybe the cook was into something illegal that involved this criminal."

"And VC found out, and Roger shot her." Joanna's stomach gurgled. "Could you bring me a couple of slices of bacon?"

"Only if you promise not to let your greasy fingers touch your dress." In a moment, Apple was back with a saucer of bacon and a cloth napkin.

Joanna chewed a slice, thinking.

"Anything else?" Apple asked.

"Just that Marquise says the police started hanging around again. Crisp wouldn't tell me anything about it." She wiped her fingers before reaching for the mascara. She didn't normally wear a lot of makeup, and she didn't want to wear much today. As she finished, she was lost in thought again.

Apple handed her the long slip, and Joanna shed her kimono and slipped the undergarment over her head, carefully pressing her lips together so not to stain the silk. Now Apple took the wedding dress from its hanger and held it open for her to step inside. Apple began fastening the long row of buttons from the bottom while Joanna started from the top. After a few, focused minutes, the dress was complete.

Apple stepped back and appraised their work. "Gorgeous." Her smile briefly clouded, and Joanna's heart twisted in sympathy. "Which shoes?"

"My silver sandals. The ones from the 1930s." Joanna took them from Apple and buckled a sandal on each foot.

All this reasoning was interesting, but it didn't explain VC's death. Why would Roger wait at the wall? She pictured the area. There was a wardrobe against that wall with a large mirror. The cook was working that night, though. It was a one-man kitchen. If he'd wanted to shoot VC, he didn't need to hide.

"Satisfied? We'd better get to Penny's. You're getting married in an hour."

"It takes only half an hour to get there."

"Better safe than sorry. Here." Apple handed her a flacon of Joy perfume.

Joanna dabbed some behind her ears and on her wrists. The sleeve's angled lace spilled over the back of her hands in a bias-cut point.

She reached for her grandmother's bracelet and clasped it on. It was a dime store bracelet dangling a single charm, but it was the closest thing to having her there.

"I need to make a call," Joanna said. Apple followed her to the living room and watched as Joanna pulled the pink princess phone to her lap and dialed a number she knew by heart: the library's reference desk. She got a recording telling her that the library was closed. Shoot. It was Sunday morning, after all.

"The library?" Apple asked.

"They're closed. Just a hunch. Thought I'd ask them about the Shanghai Tunnels. I wonder if they have any record of a tunnel connecting Marquise's and Imago Mundi?"

Joanna slipped her lipstick and powder compact into the satin drawstring bag she'd use today. She reached for her keys. The master key to Marquise's still dangled from the ring.

"How about a quick stop on the way to Penny's?"

Chapter 26

"You're kidding," Apple said. "You're getting married in an hour. Can't it wait?"

"Come to think of it, why don't we take separate cars? Then you can explain if I'm a few minutes late." Joanna was already unlocking the door. "Not that I'll be late. I'm just going to run in and check something."

"In your wedding dress? I don't have a good feeling about this."

"You know me. I won't be able to relax unless I've checked it out."

Apple stared at her. "Yes, I do know you, and I know you'll obsess. But I don't like it. People will be waiting for you. Paul won't be very happy if you don't show up."

"Come on." She pulled Apple through the door. "I'm going to show up. I'll be five or ten minutes behind you, that's all. Stop worrying."

"If you're later than that, I'm coming back for you."

"Fine. Now hurry up," Joanna said. She waved the dress's train. "I think I can drive with the train hooked to my wrist. It's light."

"You're not sitting in that car without something to protect your dress. Just a minute." Apple ran into the house and returned with a sheet. She laid it over the seat.

Joanna carefully situated herself in Old Blue and made sure the dress was completely in the car before she shut the door. She hadn't wanted Apple to know, but she was nervous about delaying the wedding, too. Not that it would be delayed much. But if she counted twenty minutes to Marquise's — traffic should be light on a Sunday morning — ten minutes poking around in the basement, she'd only allow herself that, then another twenty minutes to Penny's, well, she didn't have time to waste. If her hunch was right, now was the time to check it out. Lewis Custard would be at Penny's setting up the catering.

In a few minutes, the first guests would begin to arrive. Most of them would be Paul's family. They grew thick around Portland. Apple's family had driven down from Washington, too. Joanna's own family was sparse, and she'd come up with a cousin but hadn't been able to get in touch with her parents.

Evenings, Old Town belonged to nightclubbers, but mornings — especially weekend mornings when the few offices that had struck a claim in the neighborhood were closed for the week — belonged to street people. A van from a social service agency crawled up the street, its staff likely handing out coffee and doing safety checks. Joanna parked across from Marquise's. She knew she cut an odd figure dashing across the street in her wedding dress.

The key opened Marquise's, no trouble. She closed and locked it behind her. She stood for a moment in the theater, taking it all in. Without the distraction of a crowd and music, the smell of the building's old wood, mingling with a pine-scented cleaner, wafted from the walls and floors.

"Hello." Her voice sounded unusually loud in the silent theater. "Is anybody here?"

The theater was quiet. Every time she'd been here before, the room was full of chatter and music and laughter. The silence felt wrong.

She made her way to the basement stairwell, flicking on the light on her way down. The kitchen was eerily dark, even with the lights on, and she made sure to traverse its floor carefully to avoid Roger's fate. She felt for another light switch inside the dressing room, and the bulbs above the long stretch of mirror flickered to life. Shouldering past puffs of tulle and spandex, and ducking under a shelf of wigs before turning right, she reached the basement's far wall, where she'd found VC.

For a moment, she simply stared at the space. The floral tributes left for VC drooped and shed petals. Unconsciously, mimicking a gesture she'd seen her grandmother do thousands of times, she crossed herself.

Filling her lungs for courage, she approached the wardrobe. The wall in Roger Bing's bedroom had been only that: a wall. If there was a door here, a door that concealed illegal activity, it would explain why VC was facing away, yet had been shot face on. VC's discovery that the door existed might have been enough to get her killed. But there wasn't a door. Simply an old wardrobe.

Joanna unlatched the wardrobe to find it packed to overflowing with girdles and slips. It would be crazy to put a door in here. Who could squeeze through? Still, she lifted an armload of undergarments from the rack and laid them over a table. Now that she had enough room to maneuver, she leaned forward and felt along the wardrobe's back for a crack or something to indicate there was a door here.

She spent five precious minutes examining the wardrobe's back wall and came up empty, but for a sliver on her index finger. Plus, her sore knee was feeling the strain of leaning. After giving the wardrobe's wall a final unproductive pound with her fist, she stepped back and flexed her knee. Drat.

Well, she'd tried. Fine, she needed to get to her wedding, anyway. She replaced the undergarments on the rack and closed the wardrobe door. A playing card with Liza Minelli wearing a top hat fell from its place tucked into the mirror. She bent to replace it, and pain from her knee shot up her leg. She grabbed her knee and fell against the wardrobe.

And it slid to the right.

Joanna sucked in her breath. She righted herself and faced an old wooden door, smaller than the wardrobe that had concealed it. The door might have been a hundred years old, but the bolt that locked it was brand new.

She paused again. Paul and her guests were waiting for her at Penny's house. Would she really have the patience to go through the ceremony knowing the secret to VC's murder might be just beyond this door? She'd be late, for sure. To her own wedding. She shook her head and turned away from the wardrobe.

Surely at the dressing table she'd find something with which she could pick this lock.

Joanna followed the lock-picking rules Paul had taught her and first turned the door handle. He'd pointed out that a lot of people could save a lot of time simply by trying a lock before picking it. This one was truly locked. Next, she tried Marquise's master key, just in case this was a door he'd known about. It didn't come close to fitting the lock.

A few seconds at the dressing table and she'd assembled an impressive collection of bobby pins and wig pins. She knelt at the old door, placing a girdle under her knees to protect the lace of her wedding gown and a wig to pad her sore knee. Using a straightened bobby pin and a wig pin—these worked surprisingly well, she'd have to tell Paul—she eased the lock open, pin by pin in the tumbler. She didn't know she was holding her breath until she let it all out at once.

There. She stood and stretched her knee again, and pushed the door open. The hinges had been oiled, and the door swung silently. Beyond was Imago Mundi's basement.

Joanna thought about the crowd waiting for her at Penny's. Apple would have told them she needed to make a stop before arriving. If she spent five minutes—five minutes, that's all—looking around, she'd only be ten minutes or so late. With judicious speeding, it might only be five minutes. Then, after the ceremony, she could get in a quick call to Crisp. He'd take care of the rest.

The door opened to a short, dark hall with a cement floor and newly sheetrocked walls. The plasterboard was untaped and unpainted, and the ceiling hung low. She dropped her satin bag on the table next to the wardrobe, and unhooked the penlight attached to her key ring, slipping her keys back into her bag. Holding her breath, Joanna crept down the hall and came to a T intersection. To the right, ten or so feet down, the hall ended at the wall. To the left at a similar distance, the hall was sealed by a door.

So there were rooms here. New rooms. What were they for? Joanna halted. Whatever it was, it was worth killing for, and Roger Bing had played a role—Roger and Lewis Custard. Time was short. She should return to Marquise's and close everything up. Then again, Lewis Custard was safely out of the way. What better time than now to have a look? She'd take a quick peek in one of the rooms, that's all, then leave. Who knew? Maybe they were simply storerooms for potatoes and paper napkins.

She chose the room to her right to investigate first. A steel door locked this room. She tried the knob, and, amazingly, it opened. Her fingers went to the switch next to the door, but she dropped her hand before turning on the lights. Just in case. She lifted her penlight.

She wasn't sure what she'd been expecting, but it wasn't what she saw. The room was clean and tidy, with a linoleum floor so new that it still smelled of vinyl. Three of the room's walls were lined with tables. The thin beam from her penlight grazed the tables, rested for a moment on a filing cabinet, then stopped at a state-of-the art computer and printer. The printer's lights blinked red and green. She stepped closer. In a box next to the computer were blank passport forms. Thoughts were coming together, and she didn't like where they led. She was getting out. Now.

She closed the door behind her and retraced her steps toward Marquise's. She rounded the corner, then yanked herself back, but it was too late. He was there.

Out of the dark, a handheld light flashed on, first casting a red glow on its bearer's hand, then rising to point at her eyes. Joanna blinked against it and raised an arm as her heartbeat exploded in her chest. The light lowered, revealing Lewis Custard's face.

Chapter 27

"So nice of you to visit, Joanna," Lewis Custard said. "And so beautifully turned out, too."

Joanna was too shocked to speak. She stared ahead, willing her heart to calm. "I thought you were at the wedding."

"As the bride should be."

"Why are you here?" Joanna finally managed to say.

"Your friend mentioned you had an errand on the way to your wedding. I was afraid it might be this."

Custard was big and likely not too agile, but Joanna couldn't move quickly in the wedding dress, not to mention her sandals. Besides, he blocked the only access either up to Imago Mundi or through to Marquise's.

"Have you seen everything you wanted to see?" he asked. "Or should I give you a tour?"

"They're waiting for me. My wedding. They know I came here."

"They don't know what happened to you, except that you were kind enough to call. You thought it would be safer to deliver your message to me, naturally."

A call? She didn't want to ask.

"You had second thoughts about getting married. Too bad. The groom was crushed."

It was now or never. Joanna rushed him, turning sideways to push him with her shoulder as she'd seen football players do in high school. Custard grabbed her by the waist and threw her to the cement floor. Joanna groaned and grabbed her knee. Her sandal caught in the dress's skirt, tearing a hole in the fragile lace.

Custard yanked her up by the shoulder and hooked an arm around her neck. He marched her to the room Joanna hadn't yet explored. With his free hand, he raised the bolt barring the outside of the door before flicking on the lights. It was some sort of operating room, complete with an operating table, surgical lights, and hospital cupboards.

"People are expecting me," Joanna repeated. "They know I came here."

"If anyone thought you went anywhere, it was to Marquise's. Not here. They won't find any trace of you next door."

Would they? She'd left her purse near the wardrobe.

"Are you thinking of this, perhaps?" He pulled her satin bag from a rear pocket with one hand, keeping the other clamped on her. "I won't lie. You'd benefit from a touch of lipstick, but you won't need it here."

"What are you going to do?" She looked at the operating table with its light suspended above it, the tray of scalpels and stainless steel implements she couldn't identify.

"You'll get to visit VC soon. She'll appreciate your costume." He opened a drawer and pulled out a reel of plastic tubing.

Joanna edged to the door, but he yanked her back by the waist and pinned her to the counter. He cut an arm's length of tubing from the reel, pulled her hands behind her back, and tied them together.

"Up on the table," he said.

"No." Her voice shook. Surely he couldn't lift her.

"Up," he said with force. Before she could reply, he pushed her toward the operating table, swinging up her legs. He was more agile than he looked. As he tied her ankles, she tried kicking him against the counter. He regained his balance and threw his weight over her body. She screamed in pain as his bulk settled on her knee. He clapped a hand over her mouth. Her vision narrowed as the spasming in her knee brought her to the edge of consciousness.

Lewis Custard stood. Her ankles were now firmly bound. The false courtesy in his voice was gone. "You won't go anywhere now, and the room is soundproofed. I'm going to close up things at Marquise's and move your car. We'll see what happens next."

"They'll come," Joanna barely managed to say. The throbbing in her knee had stabilized to a steady ache. "They'll never believe I left. They'll know it was you."

He opened the door, then turned to face her. "But when I'm finished, they won't know it was you."

He turned off the lights. She heard the heft of the outside bolt as it slammed into place.

There was no doubt now. With the ID manufacturing in the next room, Custard could transform a person into anyone he wanted. He had been a plastic surgeon. No. A wave of nausea rose. The thought was too gruesome. She remembered the apartment upstairs. Once a client was transformed, he could rest there until he was completely healed. A handful of clients a year could buy a lot of maps.

Custard was at the center of the ring the police had been trying to break up, the ring that allowed criminals to arrive in Portland, then never be seen again. Here, they could get a whole new identity. Custard was planning to destroy her identity — then kill her.

Joanna lay still a moment. Paul knew she'd never run away. Didn't he? Apple must have told him where she'd gone. Maybe he'd try to find her at Marquise's. Try—and fail.

She pictured the empty bottles of champagne stacking up on the counter and the guests glancing at their watches. The drooping flowers. The tepid soup.

Figure it out. She could almost hear her grandmother whispering in her ear. Well, what tools did she have?

She was in a room with sharp instruments. She was alert and conscious, even if her knee was messed up. What she didn't have was much time. With luck, Old Blue wouldn't start right away. The car's ignition was testy. That might buy her a few minutes.

She was also bound and trapped on an operating table. That could change, at least. She swung her legs to the side, then carefully lowered her hips. She couldn't see anything—the dark absorbed light like black velvet—but the tip of her sandal touched linoleum, and she slipped to her feet.

Now what? Her hands were tied behind her back. She'd always been limber. As a kid, she used to entertain classmates by grabbing her hands behind her back and pulling them over her head. That wouldn't work now. But could she still get her hands in front by sitting on the floor and scooting back through them?

There was only one way to find out. She lowered herself to the ground and brought her bound wrists under her hind end. That part was easy, although she felt the dress rip further under the arms.

Now for the hard part. She had to fold her legs back at the knees, then slide her arms forward and over her feet. She knelt, sitting on her feet. Her knee screamed in pain. Quickly, she leaned back and forced her arms past her feet, all the while cursing the modest heels of her sandals for the extra inch she had to stretch. It felt as if her arms would be ripped from their sockets, but it worked. One success: her arms were now in front.

But she was still bound. On the floor, she could use her fingertips to pull at the tubing securing her ankles. She backed up, scooting inch by inch, to the wall and used it as a support while she stood. Then, gently hopping to save her knee from whatever pain she could, she approached the operating table, then felt her way along it.

At a mechanical click and whirr, she startled, her pulse racing. Keep calm, she told herself. It was just the heating system.

Keeping her side in contact with the operating table for guidance, she inched toward where she remembered the tray of tools. At last she bumped against it. Gingerly, she felt for a scalpel. There it was. Now she dropped to the ground—crouching was impossible—to cut the tubing from her ankles. It took a few minutes with her tied hands, but at last her feet were free. She rotated them to get the blood flowing again.

Now for her wrists. This would be trickier. She wedged the scalpel in her sandal, sharp side up, and started to work. Because the scalpel kept slipping, she cut herself once and had to will herself to return to making tiny nicks and fissures in the tubing, closer and closer together, until she was finally able to lift her wrists to her mouth and tear at the tubing with her teeth. Every few moments she stopped and listened. Was Lewis Custard coming?

Her dress was torn and probably bloodied, but at last she was free. A wave of hysteria, mixed with tears and laughter, rose in her chest. *Breathe*, she commanded herself. *Stay calm*. With delicate movements, she felt her way to the operating table and set down the scalpel. Even after all this time, there wasn't enough light for her eyes to adjust to the dark, and she didn't dare turn on the overhead fixtures to avoid alerting Custard that she was free. She might as well not have had eyes at all.

What next?

"You can do it. You're killer."

The voice seemed to come out of nowhere. Joanna squinted against the tannic dark. Did she really hear it?

A form seemed to gather in the corner of the room. A dark-skinned drag queen wearing a gold lamé Halston gown. VC. The specter's chin lifted, and she caught Joanna's gaze. Trembling, Joanna squeezed her eyes shut and opened them again. The form had vanished. Her words, "You're killer," echoed in her mind. She began to formulate a plan.

Favoring her knee, she hobbled back to the operating table. She tucked a scalpel into her bra, sharp end up. She waited.

At last, straining her ears, she heard a distant door open. She was strangely cool, almost as if she were watching herself from the room's corner. Feeling her way along the counter, she stood at the front wall, behind where the door would open.

And it was happening. The plank securing the door lifted, she heard it slide. The bolt snicked open. And now the door.

Light flooded the room, almost blinding Joanna more than the pitch dark had.

"What the—"

In a lightning move, Joanna pulled the scalpel from her bra and plunged it full force into Custard's beefy neck.

She didn't stop to see the damage. She ran. She ran toward the door sealing off this part of the basement, and, nearly crying with a mixture of relief and desperation, she clawed at the handle until it opened.

A gurgling yell and footsteps came from behind her, but she pressed ahead. *Don't look back.*

She ran past boxes of soda mix, bags of flour, racks of glasses. She threw open the door at the basement's far end and ran up the steps and burst into the Imago Mundi dining room.

"Call the police!" she yelled.

Heads swiveled toward her. She was bloodied, her hair in pieces around her dirt-stained face, her dress shredded.

"Call!" she repeated. "Now!"

The bartender reached for the phone.

Chapter 28

Detective Foster Crisp took Joanna's story quickly and efficiently. He'd sent uniformed policemen to Imago Mundi's basement to remove Lewis Custard before Joanna would venture down again. She showed him the counterfeiting and surgery rooms and the door she'd entered from Marquise's. In the surgery room, she glanced to the corner where VC had appeared, but all she saw was a dangling surgical gown.

She wouldn't have been able to do it if she didn't know Paul was on his way. As soon as the bartender had finished his call to the police, she had grabbed the phone to call Paul. She hadn't been able to read his tone. Still, she took comfort in the fact that he said he would come.

But she hadn't seen him yet. Right now, she and Crisp were in Marquise's basement. In an eerie echo of exactly a week ago, crime scene investigators were photographing the wardrobe where VC was killed.

"Is there a bathroom down here?" Crisp asked.

"Sure. Over there." Joanna pointed through the racks of show dresses to the bathroom that backed up to the kitchen.

"Let's get you cleaned up. Your boyfriend's upstairs, by the way."

For the first time in hours, Joanna's mood started to lift. "He's here? Send him down."

"Not yet," Crisp said. "Come on."

They walked through the dressing area, then cut to the left before the kitchen to arrive at the bathroom.

"Sit." Crisp pointed to the closed toilet. As Joanna lowered herself, she caught a glimpse in the mirror and did a double take. Her hair hung in strands, but that wasn't bad. It was her battered face that shocked her. Dried blood smeared one cheek, and the other was beginning to purple with bruises. She didn't even want to think about the lace wedding dress hanging in shreds from her body. Thank goodness for the slip underneath.

"Here." Crisp handed her a damp washcloth.

She took it and smiled at his kind gesture before going to work on her face. "Thank you, Crisp. You're a lifesaver, and I mean that."

"Do you need a paramedic?"

"No. I'm fine. Shaken, but fine." And very lucky to be so. "Lewis Custard is the person you've been looking for, isn't he? The person who's been changing the identities of criminals you've tracked as far as Portland?"

"It looks like it." Crisp folded his arms and leaned back against the doorjamb. "A neat operation, too. New papers, new facial patterns. He must have a post-op room upstairs where his clients could wait until they'd healed."

"That was my thought. I wouldn't be surprised if the whole top level is an apartment for his clients. Imago Mundi's security system is top-of-the-line." She remembered Custard lovingly gazing at his maps, how he was transformed touching each fragile leaf of paper. "The maps," she said.

"The what?"

"He did it to raise money to buy old maps. He showed me his collection once. He's obsessed." She rose to soak the washcloth with fresh, warm water. The heat felt so good on her skin. If only there were a deep bathtub to climb into right now.

"Could be," Crisp said. "Forensic accounting will tell us a lot. There's more investigating to do. Whether Bing killed Bo Milton or not, he was almost certainly involved in Custard's operation. We've seen people coming into Marquise's, people we've had an eye on, but we figured they were coming out as drag queens."

Joanna couldn't help but snicker. The thought of some drug lord suiting up as a female impersonator to elude the police was worthy of its own movie. To his credit, Crisp smiled, too.

"Now," Crisp continued, "my guess is that Bing let them in—probably without Marquise's knowing it—and passed them through the connecting entrance to Custard's basement. They got their new papers and their new look, and left through Imago Mundi some busy night at dinner."

"Which explains Roger's sudden bump in savings. But shoot VC?" It still seemed incomprehensible. "The cook adored Marquise. He'd never do something that would reflect poorly on the club."

"VC must have interrupted something without knowing. Maybe Bing was passing another customer through, someone unexpected."

"Had to be unexpected. It would be too risky during a show, but it would explain the odd angle she was shot at." Joanna unpinned her hair and tried to rearrange it in some semblance of tidiness. "So, Roger Bing killed VC because she could have blown the whole operation, which would have made Marquise's Showplace look even worse."

"That's about it. We'll know more after we question Custard."

"No wonder he was so freaked out when he saw VC's ghost."

Joanna's hands dropped from her hair. She faced Crisp. "He's alive, then."

Crisp didn't even blink. "Sure. You slowed him down, and he bled a lot, but he's at the station talking right now."

Joanna drew a deep breath and returned to the mirror. "Anything new on VC's mom?"

She saw his nod in the mirror. "She told the judge it was an accident, just like she told us. I wouldn't be surprised if she's out on bail Monday."

"Strange justice," Joanna said. Obsession, devotion, a mother's love—how easily passion tipped to madness.

"Agreed," Crisp said.

Joanna looked like someone washed up from a shipwreck, but at least she was clean. "Can I see Paul now?"

The hint of a smile passed his face. "All right." He turned away and murmured a few words into his cellphone. He followed her out of the bathroom, near the darkened rows of satin ruffles and silk in riotous colors. "You might as well check in with each other. Being that it's your wedding day and all."

Crisp had barely left the bathroom before Paul was down the stairs. Crisp and Paul nodded at each other as they passed.

Paul embraced Joanna with an urgency that left her breathless, then tilted her head back to inspect her face.

"You're okay?" he said.

"Fine. Now that you're here."

"You're bruised. Here, and here." His fingers brushed her cheek and shoulder.

"I'll be all right."

"Good." He still held her hard against his chest.

She pushed back enough to see his face. "You didn't really think I skipped out on the wedding, did you?"

"Of course not."

She rested against his chest again, calmer now.

"Crisp said you were all right, but I wasn't sure if he really checked. How did you get these bruises?"

Joanna took his hand and led him to the wardrobe concealing the entrance to Imago Mundi. The crime scene team had already taken photographs, and the nook was comfortably quiet. For the next ten minutes, Joanna told him the story of stopping on her way to the wedding and what followed.

He listened intently. Joanna kept becoming distracted by his crisp black suit — an early 1960s suit Apple had helped him buy. Joanna had never seen him dressed up. He was beautiful. Had he been a businessman, the occupants of acres of cubicles would have swooned over him.

"Go on," Paul urged when she lost track.

At last she came to the end of her story. "I didn't want to stay at Imago Mundi. I made them take me back here." She leaned against Paul's chest and breathed his scent.

Around the corner at the long dressing table came voices. Marquise's performers. Was it already time for the matinee show?

Joanna pulled away. "I'm sorry for messing up the wedding. What I did was so stupid. I had no idea—"

"You're safe. That's what matters."

Joanna looked at her feet a moment. Her sandals, amazingly intact, had suffered a few scrapes. She held both of Paul's hands. "I'm glad you knew I didn't run out on you."

He squeezed her again and released her. "I know you better than that. You're a fighter. If you really didn't want me, you'd have come back and told me."

"Yes," she whispered. "I mean, no — no, I wouldn't leave you, but I would have told you. You know what I mean."

He smiled. "It took only five minutes after Custard left for me to decide to come find you. Apple said you'd stopped here. I broke into Marquise's, and I found this." He held up her grandmother's bracelet. It must have broken off when she fell on the wardrobe. "I called Crisp, and he said the police were already on their way. If I'd known you were just next door, I would have found some way in."

"Paul." Something she'd been holding in check broke apart and dissolved, leaving a warm pool of emotion. "I can't believe it. It's all over." She wanted to cry, to lie down with a fluffy blanket between her and the world, to laugh with relief. "What about the guests? Were they....?" Her voice trailed off.

Conversation picked up in the dressing area. Someone — Marquise? — was humming, "Wedding Bell Blues."

"I want to talk to you about that."

"Okay." Paul's hands were elegant but strong. She ran a finger over the callus on one finger.

"We can still get married today."

She glanced up. "Today? It's hours past the ceremony. The courthouse isn't open on Sunday."

"We can get married right now. Apple and Penny loaded their cars with the leftover food." He pulled a hair away from her eyes. "We're down a few bottles of champagne."

"What about the guests?"

"Upstairs. So's the Mother Superior. She had a nap at Penny's, and she's raring to go."

Upstairs. She'd still be getting married, but upstairs. At Marquise's. Her bewilderment turned to laughter. Frenzied, ridiculous laughter. And that turned to tears. Her chest heaved with them. Paul simply held her.

She wiped her tears with Paul's handkerchief. "What about my dress?" She was still wearing shreds of 1930s lace. She lifted the torn train. "I can't get married like this."

Marquise rounded the corner. "Did somebody say 'dress'?"

Chapter 29

Half an hour later, to the recorded strains of the wedding march, Joanna climbed the stairs to Marquise's main floor.

She glimmered in the Bob Mackie design of blue and silver sequins slit up the thigh. Alexis's beautician training came in handy as she covered her bruises and created an elaborate updo studded with sequined flowers. Marquise wanted to put her in a wig, but she had to draw the line somewhere.

Summer and Marquise, in full drag, accompanied her to the stage, where Apple, her matron of honor, waited with a bouquet that was only slightly wilted. Paul was at Apple's side, and an older man she didn't recognize stood with him.

The stranger leaned over and kissed her cheek. "I'm Paul's Uncle Gene."

The Mother Superior rose from her seat and leaned on her cane. Joanna squinted into the audience.

"Put the house lights up a bit," Marquise yelled.

As if by magic, the lights over the audience rose. Joanna was filled to bursting with emotion.

"Don't cry, girl, or you'll ruin your makeup," Summer whispered. She patted Joanna's hand and took a seat with the audience, joining a row of blue habits. The Marys. Sister Mary Alberta waved discreetly. On the other side of the room, Penny beamed as if the entire ceremony were her idea. Maybe it was. She lifted a glass of champagne. Even Crisp had stayed. His silver bolo tie caught the light as he shifted on his feet.

Apple handed her peonies and lilies of the valley tied with a wide satin ribbon. Joanna lifted the bouquet to her lips and breathed the green scent of spring. Apple seemed subdued but happy. For now.

Throughout the short ceremony, Joanna's thoughts were full of Paul and the family they'd made, complete with jewel thieves, nuns, drag queens, and many less kooky but equally wonderful people. The last few years had taught Joanna a lot. One of the chief lessons was that everything good takes effort. Her life had been content and quiet when she'd met Paul and discovered a body behind the counter at Tallulah's Closet. At least, she'd thought she was content. Vintage clothing, old movies, and good meals were stop-gap food for her real drive: curiosity.

The Mother Superior talked, Joanna said the requisite "I do," and then it was time to kiss the groom.

Amazing. So amazing. A ruby the color of red currants glowed on her finger. Makeup be danged, she was going to cry. As if on cue, one of the drag queens—Hearty Burgundy?—let out a wail from the second row.

The audience cheered as Joanna and Paul walked hand in hand down the stage into the audience.

Detective Crisp pecked Joanna's cheek, then took Paul's Uncle Gene aside. The stereo system switched to the Rolling Stones singing "You Can't Always Get What You Want," and champagne corks popped.

Oh, she was happy.

Someone tapped her shoulder. She turned, her sequins throwing light on the draperies, to Uncle Gene.

"I hear you like investigating things," he said. "Let's talk later."

Afterword

Readers familiar with Portland will rightly peg Marquise's Showplace as a take on the magnificent Darcelle XV Showplace. Thank you to Darcelle and her performers, Summer Seasons and Alexis Campbell Starr, for letting me riff on the cabaret. All the goodness, fun, and love I describe is real. The murders and secret passageways aren't. (Also, I can't think of a single drag family named after jug wine.)

Similarly, thank you to the owners and staff of the Holman Funeral Home, an inspiration for the Milton Funeral Home. What a magnificent building and smart, friendly staff.

As always, I owe a huge debt of gratitude to the members of my writing group, Cindy Brown, Evan Lewis, Doug Levin, Ann Littlewood, and Marilyn McFarlane; second reader Robin Remmick; copyeditor extraordinaire Raina Glazener; and cover designer Ebooklaunch.

CPSIA information can be obtained
at www.ICGtesting.com
Printed in the USA
BVHW071524150119
537843BV00003B/363/P

9 780990 413370